She Felt So Alive!

Her cheeks flushed in anticipation and excitement. Her eyes sparkled. Julianne actually looked like her glamorous twin sister! It wasn't just features— those were identical. It was more attitude. This was without a doubt the wildest thing she'd ever done. It was pure fantasy; she couldn't keep up this pretense for more than a little while. For once in her life she planned to experience the adventures her sister took for granted.

No one would be hurt. As long as she kept it firmly in mind that this was only a fantasy. When her vacation ended, she'd return to the library, to her small town. But that was weeks away. For now, she was free and about to spend the day with the sexiest man she'd ever seen....

Dear Reader,

Silhouette Desire is proud to launch three brand-new, emotional and romantic miniseries this month! We've got twin sisters switching places, sexy men who rise above their pasts and a ranching family marrying off their Texas daughters.

Along with our spectacular new miniseries, we're bringing you Anne McAllister's latest novel in her bestselling CODE OF THE WEST series, July's MAN OF THE MONTH selection, *The Cowboy Crashes a Wedding.* Next, a shy, no-frills librarian leads a fairy-tale life when she masquerades as her twin sister in Barbara McMahon's *Cinderella Twin,* book one of her IDENTICAL TWINS! duet. In *Seducing the Proper Miss Miller* by Anne Marie Winston, the town's black sheep and the minister's daughter cause a scandal with their sudden wedding.

Sexy Western author Peggy Moreland invites readers to get to know the McCloud sisters and the irresistible men who court them—don't miss the first TEXAS BRIDES book, *The Rancher's Spittin' Image.* And a millionaire bachelor discovers his secret heir in *The Tycoon's Son* by talented author Shawna Delacorte. A gorgeous loner is keeping quiet about *His Most Scandalous Secret* in the first book in Susan Crosby's THE LONE WOLVES miniseries.

So get to know the friends and families in Silhouette Desire's hottest new miniseries—and watch for more of their love stories in months to come!

Regards,

Melissa Senate

Melissa Senate
Senior Editor
Silhouette Books

BARBARA McMAHON
CINDERELLA TWIN

SILHOUETTE *Desire*®

Published by Silhouette Books

America's Publisher of Contemporary Romance

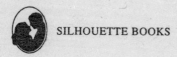

SILHOUETTE BOOKS

ISBN 0-373-76154-6

CINDERELLA TWIN

Printed in U.S.A.

Books by Barbara McMahon

Silhouette Desire

One Stubborn Cowboy #915
Cowboy's Bride #977
Bride of a Thousand Days #1017
Boss Lady and the Hired Hand #1072
Santa Cowboy #1116
*Cinderella Twin #1154

Silhouette Romance

Sheik Daddy #1132

*Identical Twins!

BARBARA McMAHON

was born and raised in the South. She traveled around the world while working for an international airline, then settled down to raise a family and work for a computer firm. She began writing when her children started school. Now that she has been fortunate enough to realize her long-held dream of quitting her "day job" and writing full-time, she and her husband have moved from the San Francisco Bay Area to California's Sierra Nevada. With the beauty of the mountains visible from her windows, and the pace of life slower, she finds more time than ever to think up stories and share them with others. Readers can write to Barbara at P.O. Box 977, Pioneer, CA 95666-0977.

To my "twin," Suzanne Coleburn,
one of the Belles of Romance—
hope you enjoy!

One

Envy is a terrible thing, Julianne Bennet thought as her gaze scanned the front of the huge glass-and-wood structure. Fumbling for money, she paid the cabdriver and lifted her bag. Maybe she could be excused for feeling just a twinge, she mused as she walked up the flagstone path. Her eyes took in the casual landscaping, the weathered siding and the open expanse of windows. The enormous house sat solidly on the bluff above the sea—nothing like her own petite cottage in Virginia.

The air mingled the spicy scent of the rich red carnations growing against the wood siding with that tangy hint of the sea. She heard the muffled crash of breakers, but the house blocked her view of the beach. From the side, she could see the deep blue of the Pacific Ocean stretching beyond the house to the horizon.

What a difference from Charlottesville, she mused as she rang the bell, thinking of her cottage behind the Morgans's house. The Blue Ridge Mountains of Virginia were a world away from the beaches of Malibu, California.

"Julianne! I can't believe you actually came! You should have called me from the airport, I would have come to pick you up." The woman who was her mirror image reached out to hug her, then held her at arm's length while she studied each feature. Her own face lit with excitement.

"I asked if I could come, why are you surprised?" Julianne said, almost laughing in giddy delight. Her smile matched that of her twin's. "It's odd to see someone who looks just like me yet dresses so differently. If we dressed alike, maybe it wouldn't seem so strange. Gosh, it's good to see you!"

Jackie du Marcel wore a slinky bright yellow silk jumpsuit that hugged her figure, draping curves and valleys that matched Julianne's. Her brown hair, as short as Julianne's, looked tousled and windblown, and a lot more exotic than Julianne's neat style. Julianne's conservative slacks and cotton sweater made her feel downright dowdy next to her glamorous twin.

"I can't believe how long it's been since we got together. Letters are fine, but this is better. I guess I wasn't totally convinced you'd show up. God, it's good to see you! Come in. Is that all you brought, one bag? I never travel anywhere without three or four. And if I'm going somewhere for several weeks it could be more." Jackie talked rapidly, her hands gesturing as if punctuating her words.

Julianne laughed and stepped inside. Glancing around, she noted the modern furniture, all leather and chrome, the polished wooden floors, and the wide expanse of windows that seemed to bring the sea right into the house.

"Oh, Jackie, this is great!" Dropping the suitcase, Julianne crossed the room to the sliding-glass doors and gazed out. "Imagine having this view every day. How do you ever leave it?"

"Yeah, I like it." Joining her twin, Jackie slid open the door. "Come on the deck, it's even better. I can't believe you haven't come to visit before. We should have made plans long ago. I should have insisted."

The setting sun blazed on the horizon, a fiery ball of reddish orange in the late afternoon sky. As far as Julianne could see, the peaceful Pacific Ocean shimmered in golds and yellows, reflecting the final rays of the day. The brisk breeze that blew from the water carried a hint of salt spray. To her right, gulls cavorted in midair, crying their plaintive wails as they swooped on the wind. For the first time in ages Julianne felt totally free.

"I had so much going on before, the timing wasn't good," she said slowly, wondering for the millionth time why she and her sister didn't get together regularly. Jackie could afford to come to Virginia anytime she wanted. Of course the quiet little college town probably held no interest for her glamorous jet-setting twin. She didn't blame her for staying away, but wished she had visited at least once in the past few years.

"And now is a good time?" Jackie asked.

Julianne sighed. "It won't get any better."

"If you like it here so much, maybe you could move out. It would be great to live near each other. We missed a lot as kids. Twins should grow up together. Think of the havoc we could have wrought," Jackie said, her eyes twinkling.

Julianne turned and studied her sister. "I'm not planning to move. Actually, I'll probably go home and marry David."

"Ouch. The dentist? Thought that's what you didn't want. Your call sounded almost frantic."

"Maybe I overreacted. He's a very nice man," she said primly.

"Honey, nice men are a dime a dozen. But does he ring your chimes?"

Julianne shrugged. She didn't like discussing David behind his back. They'd been friends for years, casually dating, spending their free time together. But she had not expected his proposal. She couldn't understand when his change of interest had happened. Could she have done something to delay it, or had his proposal been inevitable? It certainly wasn't his fault she felt uncertain about her future. Something seemed missing, but she couldn't identify exactly what.

"We've been friends for years, but he doesn't ring any chimes," Julianne admitted reluctantly. Was that the missing piece, no bell-ringing?

"Then hold off, honey, until you find someone who does," Jackie advised.

"Like you did?" Julianne asked slyly.

Jackie laughed and shook her head.

"Jean was wonderful. I was crazy about him and he about me. But we just burned out. Too much, too fast, I guess. But he rang chimes like Quasimodo! And we have a friendly enough divorce. We still enjoy each other's company when our paths cross."

Julianne didn't ask what enjoying each other's company entailed—she could imagine. Probably exactly what she'd do if she had a French playboy ex-husband.

She smiled at the sister she hadn't seen in more years than she wished to count. Of course, they had not been raised together. Still, they should have managed more meetings than they had.

"When do you leave?" Julianne asked.

"In the morning. I'll only be gone a week or so, two tops. I can't believe the timing. Two days ago the schedule called for me to leave in a month. Then the studio contacted me to say they were rearranging the filming sequence because Miss Adams got sick and I have to get there right away. Then your call came. I thought you might not come if you knew I wouldn't be here the entire time. But I don't want you to leave—plan to stay right here. I'll be back as soon as I can."

"They're filming in Mexico?"

"Yeah, down on the Yucatán. When the lead actress got sick, they decided to continue filming as much as they could of the other scenes—to keep from interrupting or delaying the schedule. We'll film all my part, then I'll be back."

"I think it's wonderful you're in another movie."

"Just a bit part, Jules, nothing like the leads Dad gets. I'm restless, can't settle on anything. I've been a bit player in a couple of other movies and would love to have a stronger role, but I don't want to make this my life. I don't know what I want to do. But the filming won't take long, then I'll be back and we'll do the town!"

"Nice—even if it is bit parts."

"Perks of being the daughter of Steven Bennet."

For a moment the old hurt resurfaced in Julianne. She, too, was the daughter of Steven Bennet, but there had been no perks for her. Their famous movie star father had waltzed out of her life when he'd divorced their mother. Each parent had taken a child to raise. While her mother made an effort to keep in touch with Jackie, her father only remembered he had a second daughter on her birthday and at Christmas. A hasty call to make sure she was doing all right was about as involved as Steven managed. Sometimes she suspected his presents were purchased by a secretary. No notes ever accompanied the gifts, no invitations to come visit had ever been issued. Only vague promises to get together "soon."

She touched the wooden railing, leaning over a bit to study the path that led to the top of the bluff. There must be a way down to the beach. Afraid her sister might pick up on her anger, she concentrated on the sandy path. It had not been fair. She, too, would have enjoyed experiencing some of the glamorous life Jackie took for granted. Would it have hurt Steven Bennet to invite his other daughter out once in a while for a visit?

"You okay?" Jackie asked, touching her lightly on the shoulder.

"Sure." It wouldn't do to complain to Jackie. It wasn't her fault. They'd been seven when their parents divorced. Julianne still remembered the heartbreak of being separated from her sister, her twin, seventeen years ago. But Jackie had had no more say in the arrangement than she had. And it was all water under the bridge now.

Smiling, Julianne met her sister's gaze.

"I'm dying to see the house. Show me around?"

"Come on. I love it—purchased it with my divorce settlement. It's just what I wanted."

Jackie had done all right as a result of the divorce from her former husband, French playboy Jean Antoine du Marcel.

As they wandered through the large house Julianne couldn't help thinking that Jackie appeared far wealthier than Julianne would ever be. Jackie moved in socially exalted circles, a darling of the Hollywood crowd, a friend of numerous high-placed government officials, and the sweetheart of the posh jet-setters of the French Riviera, thanks to Jean and their celebrity father.

Wistfully Julianne listened as Jackie recounted where she'd purchased her paintings, or the statue that graced one table. The whole house seemed more like a movie set than a home. Yet Jackie fit in perfectly. It suited her.

When the tour ended, Jackie put Julianne's suitcase in the master bedroom. "I'll be gone, so you might as well enjoy the room. The bath has a whirlpool feature and staying in here beats traipsing through the hallway to use the tub. Besides, it's my favorite room and I know you'll love it, too."

And Julianne did. Two walls were almost solid glass, which gave her the feeling of being outdoors. The huge bathroom seemed larger than her cottage living room, and the whirlpool tub was big enough to accommodate an intimate party of eight.

As Jackie helped her put her clothes away in the walk-in closet, a bit of envy touched Julianne when she viewed the wardrobe her sister had acquired. Wild and bold—the styles and colors were vastly different from Julianne's usual conservative attire. Lovingly she fingered one of the gowns.

"Help yourself to anything you want. We must be the same size. You're not in Virginia now, live a little," Jackie offered carelessly with a quick glance at her sister's clothes.

Julianne shook her head. "I don't think these are quite me."

"Why not give them a try—live it up!"

"Everything about you seems different," Julianne said slowly, drawing the dress from the hanger and holding it up in front of her. "Your entire way of life is so foreign to mine. I think I envy you sometimes."

Jackie laughed. "It's the grass-is-greener syndrome, Jules. I feel that way about you. You have a close relationship with Mom that I've never had. I hardly know our brothers and sister. And there is a timelessness about living in a small town, having traditions and values that go back to the founding fathers." She shrugged sheepishly and grinned. "Sometimes I envy what you have."

"Want to switch?" Julianne asked and flashed a mischievous smile. She was surprised to learn her sister didn't seem as satisfied with her own life as Julianne had thought she'd be.

Jackie shook her head. "Can't this week, I have to go to Mexico. But you can enjoy what I have, pretend anything you want. You're on vacation, indulge. You might even change your mind about David—the—Dentist. Hold out for a chime-ringer."

Slowly Julianne wandered to stand in front of the full-length mirror that lined one wall, imagining what she'd look like wearing the dress, how she'd feel. For one daring moment she let her imagination soar. To pretend to be Jackie, to wear the fancy clothes her sister wore with such insouciance, to drive the candy-apple-red Mustang convertible she'd seen in the garage, to mingle with Hollywood's elite—it sounded wonderful. And a total change for a quiet librarian from Charlottesville, Virginia. Dare she take her sister up on her suggestion? Even for a day or so?

The next evening Julianne twirled around on the deck, smoothing her hands over the sensuous silk of the jade green jumpsuit. She felt deliciously wicked in the creation. She'd never owned anything remotely like it and probably never would. But for the next few days she could splurge to her heart's delight in a hundred different outfits as sexy and sensuous as this.

Julianne sank into one of the chairs scattered around the deck. She placed her bare feet on the lower rung of the wooden railing, scooting down in the chair slightly as she let the beauty of the early evening soak into her, soothe her. Jackie had left that morning for Mexico and Julianne had indulged herself by spending the rest of the day on the beach. The umbrella her sister had provided had kept her shaded for the most part, but enough reflected rays had managed to sneak through to turn her skin a light golden brown. Now, as she enjoyed the sunset, she felt peacefully alone at the edge of the world.

The homes in Malibu Beach were few and far apart. People who lived in Malibu paid for privacy and got it. The place to her right was barely visible beyond the huge boxwood hedge that separated the two properties. "The Arunsons are on a cruise on the *QEII*. They won't be home until July," Jackie had casually mentioned during yesterday's house tour. "Nice couple, older and wealthy as sin."

Then, waving her hand casually toward the house to the left, "Cade is in Italy someplace. He sold some Italian studio a license for his software and they botched it up. He does special effects, you know." Julianne had briefly glanced out the bedroom window at the time toward the traditional Spanish-style home next door.

Julianne smiled as she recalled how her sister had so offhandedly mentioned her neighbors and their travels. If one of her Charlottesville neighbors had left for a cruise, the entire town would have known and discussed it for days.

With both neighbors gone, she had the whole expanse of beach, sea and sky to herself. In another few moments the sun would sink completely behind the horizon and twilight would cloak the coast. The balmy air stirred the wisps of hair around her cheeks. The gulls were quiet, the murmur of the surf a constant companion.

She sighed in pleasure. Tomorrow she'd lie on the beach again or maybe try that sports car along the twisting roads that led to Los Angeles. Knowing she wouldn't drive that splashy red car with the breathtaking speed her sister enjoyed, she would still get plenty of excitement from the powerful vehicle. She wished she could drive it home. Wouldn't the boys drool if they had a chance to ride in it? Both of her half-brothers were on the verge of learning to drive and consequently car mad. Before she left, she'd have to get a picture to show them what they'd missed.

Jackie's comment echoed in her mind—she was on vacation, make the most of it. Idly daydreaming, Julianne considered doing just that. She could wear the bold and dashing clothes her sister favored, drive her car. Pretend that this was her life, a huge house on the edge of forever. She would shed her own rather prim style, forget she lived a quiet existence in a college town wondering if life was passing her by. For the next few days she could pretend to be Jackie du Marcel, femme fatale, living on the West Coast. Accountable to no one, free to do just what she wanted!

With that, Julianne laughed at her nonsense and went inside to prepare her dinner. She had as much chance of living like Jackie as she had of flying to Paris tomorrow. Still, she thought wistfully, it would be fun to see how the other half lived.

After a solitary meal, she drew a warm bath in the whirlpool and relaxed with a good mystery in the sybaritic splendor. Finally giving in to fatigue, she snuggled down in Jackie's large bed. It was early, not yet ten. But she hadn't adjusted to West Coast time yet. She could scarcely stay up beyond nine, and awoke with the birds. So much for life in the fast lane.

Cade Marshall dropped the flight bags inside his front door and ran his hand behind his neck, trying to ease some of the stress and fatigue that gripped him. Damn, he should have stayed over in New York. Trips from Europe straight to the West Coast were killers. He had passed dead tired a few hours ago, yet if he went to bed now as the sun rose, he'd wake up as it set and have to adjust tomorrow. Might as well bite the bullet today. If he could make it until late afternoon, he'd sleep until morning and quickly readjust to California time.

His house felt hot and stuffy. Hadn't the cleaning service followed his instructions about airing it out? He had faxed them day before yesterday—Italian time—that he would be home today.

Hungry and roaming the kitchen, he slammed a cupboard door. The service he'd hired sure as hell hadn't lived up to its reputation. There was nothing to eat in the house. Not even instant coffee to give him a much needed caffeine fix. Damn!

He rubbed his dry eyes, his hand moving to his jaw to scratch the day-old beard. He needed caffeine or bed, and while bed sounded more appealing, he refused to give in to fatigue.

Coffee, industrial strength and enough to float a battleship, would wake him up enough to read his mail and unpack. A swim later would keep sleep at bay. He looked at the house next door, it was a lot closer than driving back into town. Everything was still. Was Jackie even home? Sleeping if she were. Well, neighbors were supposed to be helpful, and it was high time he tapped into some help. He rummaged around in his drawer and found the house key. Whistling softly, he crossed the yard separating their houses and knocked quietly on the door. After several minutes, he let himself in.

He'd come over a few times during the two years they'd been next-door neighbors, sometimes to share a meal, other times to borrow something. He didn't think Jackie would mind if he helped himself to some coffee. He sauntered into the kitchen and pulled the beans from the refrigerator, noticing that she had apparently just gone shopping—her refrigerator was full.

He hesitated once he had the bag in hand. Maybe he'd use

her machine. He'd make enough coffee to keep himself awake until evening, and brew an extra cup or two for Jackie. Have it ready for her when she awoke as thanks for lending him some. If he felt energetic enough after he had a few sips, he'd even make breakfast. They'd shared breakfast a few times—enough for him to know how she liked her eggs. And if she wasn't awake by the time he finished cooking, he would make it breakfast in bed. Wouldn't that surprise the hell out of her?

Of course he'd have to find her bedroom first. He'd never been upstairs.

Cade poured the hot strong coffee in his cup. The aroma alone issued a wake-up call. He added a heaping teaspoon of sugar, not for the sweetness, but for the extra energy—running on low, he needed all the help he could get to stay awake.

He burned his mouth with his first gulp, yet waited only a couple of seconds before taking another.

Cup raised to his lips, he paused when he heard something. Smiling, he sipped again. Jackie must be stirring. The fragrance of the coffee probably woke her. He glanced at his watch, not even seven. She was going to be royally annoyed.

Stepping warily into the doorway, Julianne came to a halt, startled to see a man leaning against the counter casually sipping coffee and looking right at home. The pot in the coffeemaker was almost full. Since the tantalizing aroma had awakened her, that was no surprise. Studying him gravely, her heart pounded. Who was he? Obviously someone who knew her sister well enough to make himself at home.

"Morning, Jack," he said, raising the cup in salute. "Want a cup?"

Julianne nodded, in shock. *He thought she was Jackie!* Yesterday after Jackie had left, Julianne had played the part of her sister by dressing up in her clothes, wandering through the house, imagining how exciting Jackie's life must be. Now this morning a friend of her sister's actually thought she was Jackie! Amazed, she remained in the doorway, wondering who he was. A close friend, by the nickname, by the ease in which he made himself at home. Just how close?

She could tell he was tall, even slouched against the counter. Tall, dark and handsome. What a cliché—yet in this case totally true. He either lived at the beach or spent a fortune in a tanning salon. His skin was a deep dark tan, the kind that came from sailing or surfing all summer. His dark hair, which fell forward with no regard to style, grew thick and shaggy, yet because of it, holding a certain appeal. She wanted to brush the errant strands off his forehead, see if they could be tamed. Startled at the intensity of that desire, she clenched her hands into fists. She didn't even know the man, where had that wild thought come from?

Meeting his gaze, she discovered startling green eyes. She expected brown. Julianne couldn't think of anyone she knew with green eyes. His shone like emeralds, brilliant, deep, and sparkling with vitality as they calmly surveyed her over the rim of a coffee cup.

Realizing his gaze skimmed her at a leisurely pace, she looked down to make sure her robe was fastened. She'd grabbed it in a hurry when she thought she heard something, or someone, downstairs. Touching the floor, the prim yellow terry-cloth robe was nothing like the lacy confections she'd seen in her sister's closet.

"You're buttoned from tip to toe. Why the modesty? Is this the real you when you aren't playing glamour queen?" he asked casually, his eyes studying her.

"I wasn't expecting anyone," she said slowly, stalling for time. She had promised herself she'd fling caution to the wind and enjoy this vacation, be as wild as she liked. Now suddenly someone who knew her sister mistook her for Jackie. Dare she play the role of her sister for a few minutes—like a part in a movie? The challenge tantalized, the notion wild and outrageous. She knew they looked alike, but could she fool one of her sister's friends, even for a little while? Or would she blow it as soon as she opened her mouth?

Trying to imagine what her twin would do, Julianne stared at him while she thought of and discarded a dozen ideas. To begin with, Jackie wouldn't wear a floor-length terry robe. Not if the nothing-confections upstairs were her usual attire. Her heart began to pound as she considered continuing the charade. Maybe she could do it. And if she was discovered, who would she hurt? Embarrass herself a bit, perhaps, but nothing more.

He tilted his head, his expression giving nothing away. Slowly he raised the cup and drank again, his eyes never leaving hers.

"I just got in," he said.

"From?" she asked. Jackie would know. Of course, Jackie would know him and not need to question him. She felt as if she were crossing a pond of ice, fearful of breaking through and plunging into water over her head. Dare she find out how good she was at acting? Did that talent run in the family? Then again, maybe her idea of pretending to be Jackie was stupid. Who did she really think she could fool? Despite their looks, they were nothing alike.

"Europe," he said impatiently.

God, this wasn't Jean, was it? The only picture she'd seen of her brother-in-law had been blurred as he'd been turning when it was snapped. But Jean was tall with dark hair. Jackie's ex-husband would know in two seconds she wasn't his former wife. Suddenly the daring thoughts of stepping into Jackie's shoes seemed childish and foolish. How could she pretend to be Jackie du Marcel? Much as she might enjoy life in the fast lane for a week or two, there was too much she didn't know about her sister to fool anyone. Like who this gorgeous man was for starters and why he felt he had a right to invade Jackie's kitchen at—

She glanced at the clock. It wasn't even seven!

He noticed her look and smiled. "Early for you. I'm surprised you got up."

Slowly she looked at him again. She wished he would stop staring at her. Her skin tingled and felt too tight. She didn't like the sensation, yet didn't know how to stop feeling so...so aware of him as a *man*. Or herself as a woman. He needed a shave, and she wanted to run her fingertips over the roughness of his beard. His clothes were wrinkled, as if he'd slept in them. He looked tired, leaning against the counter. And she wanted to offer him a bed.

A bed?

To rest in, not to—

She took a breath, she couldn't just blurt out that she didn't know him. Yet if she didn't find out soon, she would give herself away.

"Aren't you going to give me a big kiss hello?" he asked softly, amusement lurking beneath his tone, showing in his eyes. He didn't move. Sprawled against her counter, his legs spread to hold him, the cup again tilted against his lips, he looked as blatantly masculine as any man she'd ever come in contact with. She wasn't used to men like this. Was he typical of California men? Or was he Jean Antoine du Marcel? She had never met her sister's husband. They had married hurriedly, no time for a fancy wedding, to their mother's dismay.

And of course Jackie never came to Charlottesville, so the family had not met her husband before the divorce. There had been no need once they had separated.

Did he really expect a kiss? Licking suddenly dry lips, her gaze moved to his mouth. His lips quirked in a half smile. For a second Julianne wondered what they'd feel like against hers.

She snapped her gaze back to his, and shook her head. "In your dreams!"

He threw back his head and laughed, the sound rich and infectious. His eyes danced in amusement. "For a moment I almost thought you'd call my bluff," he said.

She shook her head again, giving thanks for a touch of sanity. But the longing to offer a kiss remained strong.

His green eyes blazed down at her as she stepped a bit closer to him. She felt his male heat, breathed in a disturbingly erotic male scent. She took a deep breath, held it as her eyes searched his. Slowly he put his cup on the counter, never moving his gaze from hers. The amusement in his eyes confused her. Was she behaving totally foreign to Jackie?

Striving for some composure, hoping he didn't see how wobbly her knees felt or notice the stain of color in her cheeks, she smiled and shrugged. "Have a good trip?" Her heart beat rapidly as she frantically tried to think as her sister would; to act like a cosmopolitan jet-setter who knew how to handle a man as dangerous as this one.

"People don't go to work on software snafus to have a good trip. It would have been cheaper and easier to devise the special effects they needed and forget about their doing it themselves. But, yes, the trip went okay. The food was great. Italian hotels leave a lot to be desired, however."

This was Jackie's neighbor, the one she'd said would be gone for weeks. The relief he wasn't Jean coursed through her in a tangible wave. But she wasn't safe yet. What was his name? Stalling, hoping she never had to call him by name, she poured herself a cup of coffee and went to perch on the edge of a chair at the table set in the bay window. From here she had a fantastic view of the ocean.

The kitchen came furnished with all the gadgets and equipment for a gourmet cook. Did her sister cook? Somehow they had never discussed it. The cupboards were stocked with food, as was the refrigerator, most of the food acquired last night after dinner. They had eaten at a quiet little restaurant, then Jackie had driven to the huge supermarket that remained open all night. Shopping for groceries at eleven o'clock at night had been a novelty, Julianne thought. And the way Jackie had questioned her on every item had her wondering if Jackie expected Julianne to do the cooking while she visited. How odd to know so little about her own twin.

"You're home earlier than planned, aren't you?" she asked, trying desperately to remember everything her sister had said about this neighbor.

"Pete's still over there, but we found the problem right

away. They shouldn't have messed with the basic software. Want me to fix breakfast?''

Julianne looked up at that, surprised.

''If you hadn't come down, I planned to serve you in bed,'' he said audaciously, grinning. ''If I found your room, that is.''

''I can fix it.''

''Then hop to it, Jack. I'm starving.''

''Inviting yourself over?''

He drained his cup and replaced it on the counter. ''No food at my place. You'd think that new service would provide better for their customers. I don't think highly of your recommendation. And don't tell me I need to give them a chance. They had one and blew it. If they can't handle the job, they should not misrepresent themselves in their advertising. I'll look for someone else.''

''You might try asking them why they didn't do what you wanted and give them a chance to explain,'' Julianne said as she rose and headed for the refrigerator, glad for something to do. It was obvious the man didn't plan to leave anytime soon. He fascinated her. She wanted to learn more about him, but should she continue this charade? Sooner or later he would discover she wasn't Jackie, and she would probably feel like a total idiot.

He stared hard at her for a long moment. Finally he nodded and looked away. ''Yes, I guess I could. Not taking umbrage at my opinion about your recommendation?''

Obviously Jackie would. Julianne shrugged her shoulders and remained silent.

''I want French toast,'' he said as he pulled a chair from the table and sat down, rocking back on two legs. ''And don't burn it.''

Did that answer her question about her sister's cooking? Who burned French toast?

''Have any meat—bacon or ham?'' he asked.

Julianne scanned the contents of the refrigerator. She remembered Jackie buying a package of bacon and found it in the meat drawer. She loved bacon, yet rarely indulged. Her mother prided herself on being a nutrition freak and insisted her children eat only the best, which meant low-fat, low-calorie foods. Julianne lived on her own, but still followed many of her mother's dictates in food. Some habits were hard to break.

But she was on vacation, she reminded herself, time to do things differently. She was three thousand miles from anyone who knew her. Why not?

"What have you been up to lately?" he asked when Julianne began to soak the bread in egg batter.

For an instant she froze. It was one thing to play at being her sister when it involved merely wearing her clothes or driving her car. But to convincingly impersonate Jackie around her friends would probably be impossible. And from what she'd seen of her sister since arriving, Jackie would laugh at her feeble masquerade. Yet she wasn't ready to admit that she was Julianne. Smiling, Julianne tossed her head and glanced at him over her shoulder with what she hoped would pass as a provocative smile.

"I've been busy—shopping, dancing, the usual." She hadn't a clue what her sister did for "the usual," but maybe he would.

"Want to go out tonight to dinner?" he asked easily. "We can go to that restaurant we tried a few months ago. I won't be much company, I'm so tired from traveling I can hardly see straight, but I promise to stay awake long enough to eat."

She hesitated. Not a good idea, spending more time with this man. Sooner or later he was sure to catch on.

"Hot date?" he asked when she didn't respond.

She shook her head, trying desperately to come up with an excuse to avoid dinner.

"Then say yes and cook breakfast. I'm hungry."

"Okay. What should I wear?"

He looked puzzled for a moment. "What you usually wear, I guess. It's just dinner at Garcia's."

"Right." She flipped the bread into the pan. What did Jackie usually wear? Was Garcia's some posh restaurant that would take four hours to work through a meal, or some trendy place where they'd meet dozens of friends? She was crazy to even try this. She had to tell him. Yet, embarrassment froze her tongue. How in the world would she explain without looking like the world's biggest fool?

"Are you all right, Jackie?" Cade asked.

"Of course, why?" She flipped a piece of batter-coated bread, afraid to turn around.

"You seem different, somehow. Not like yourself."

"I...uh, I think I'm coming down with a cold," she quickly improvised.

"What you need is a day lying in the sun, bake out the germs. We can go out later and laze around the beach all day and I'll tell you about my trip."

She piled the golden-brown French toast on a plate, added several strips of crisp bacon and turned to hand it to him. He stood right beside her. She almost tipped the plate down the front of him. "Oh."

"Thanks, looks better than last time." He reached around her to open a cupboard door, almost encircling her with his body and his arm. He crowded against her as he reached for something. Julianne gave way until she pressed against the counter. Paralyzed, she couldn't move, her legs wouldn't respond. Breathing in the scent of bacon, cinnamon and tantalizing male, her eyes traced his jaw, the brown column of his throat. Every nerve ending in her body tingled as he leaned in against her. The plate was the only thing that separated them. She swallowed hard, her eyes on his mouth. Her knees threatened to buckle. She might not be able to move away, but she might just sink into a puddle right in front of him.

Her imagination soared. What would it be like to be flirtatious like her sister, wild and uninhibited? To kiss him, to have him kiss her?

Two

"Need syrup," Cade said, pulling out the bottle.

Released from the spell that bound her, Julianne gently shoved the plate against him, slid to one side and put some distance between them. She tried to control the wayward trend of her thoughts as she dipped bread for her own French toast, her terry-cloth sleeve almost slipping into the egg batter. She'd taken no time to brush her hair when she heard the noise in the kitchen. She felt as glamorous as a slug. Taking a deep breath, Julianne tried to get her raging hormones under control despite the devilishly gorgeous man sitting at the kitchen table.

"Wear that crochet thingy," he said as he placed his plate on the table and plopped the bottle of syrup beside it.

Julianne glanced at him. What 'crochet thingy'? A cover-up for the beach?

"It's at the cleaners," she said, stalling again. Maybe she should just turn and tell him that—

"You sent a bathing suit to the cleaners?"

A crocheted bikini? Her sister obviously ran a bit wilder in her attire than she had suspected. "Oh, that, uh, I don't know where it is. I thought you meant..." She trailed off.

Julianne waited for her toast to brown, wondering how she could manage to keep up the impersonation when she felt constantly at a loss. What had seemed like a fun-filled idea moments ago now proved to be extremely stressful in implementation. She should just tell him she was Jackie's sister and let the chips fall where they may. Maybe she could pretend to be sleepwalking. Cocking her head to one side, she wondered if she could pull that off. Acting proved harder than she imagined, especially without a script. Yet each minute that she succeeded in impersonating her sister gave her a bit more confidence.

"Want some more coffee?" she asked, picking up the pot, holding it poised over his empty mug, hoping he wouldn't pursue the crocheted bathing suit. She wished she could ask how well he knew her sister. Was there something more between the two of them than neighbors? Did Jackie consider this man a friend? Wistfully she compared her friendship with David. She couldn't imagine having breakfast so casually with him, and she'd known him for years. When David had asked her to marry him, she'd been stunned. Of course he'd kissed her over the years, but nothing more. And she had never felt the same kind of physical awareness that bubbled over this morning.

"Sure." He reached for the mug when she handed it to him. His fingers brushed hers in a deliberate caress. Julianne almost dropped the pot. Unused to such blatant sexuality in every gesture, she didn't know how to respond—ignore him, or flirt back. The men she knew were friendly, yet respectful. *And she knew their names!* Desperately she tried to remember what her sister had said about the man. He did something with special effects. What else had Jackie said?

"Thought you were hoping for a part in some new movie. Did it fall through?" he asked as she sat gingerly across from him.

"No. I mean, yes, it fell through."

"Just wondered if you wanted to practice the reading with me like you did last time. I need something to get involved in, to stay awake today." He ate with relish, appeared to enjoy every morsel.

"Thanks. I don't need to do that." Lie upon lie. She never knew she had such a talent. Her mother would be horrified. Her brothers would never let her hear the end of it should they ever find out. Jackie would probably egg her on. Good heavens, maybe acting did run in the family.

Sighing softly, Julianne tried to think up ways to admit to her deception without having the man think less of her. What grown woman played such childish games? Yet the excitement led her on. She wondered if she could hold her own with this man, with any of Jackie's other friends. Or would they find her hopelessly provincial. She had not had the benefit of travel as Jackie had, but she had her books and her vivid imagination. She read voraciously, and rather thought she could hold her own.

Pleased with the enthusiasm with which he attacked the meal, she ate quietly, wishing she'd spent more time with Jackie to learn how her sister would have reacted around this man. She suspected Jackie would flirt for all she was worth. She had done so with strangers at the supermarket, so why wouldn't she with a neighbor?

Despite her best intentions of sampling life in the fast lane, Julianne didn't think she could bring herself to flirt with the man seated opposite her. When he finished his French toast, he'd eat her up in two bites. She glanced at him from beneath her lashes and found his gaze directed on her. He needed a haircut, but the longish hair looked good on him. The faint lines around his eyes were due to fatigue, not age. He looked to be not much more than thirty.

Watching as he ate, she again experienced that almost-overwhelming desire to brush her fingertips against that beard-roughened jaw, to feel the texture of his skin against hers.

Would he pull her into his arms and demand a kiss if she gave in to the temptation? Or think she was out of her mind?

"Do you need anything?" she asked nervously, conscious of him sitting so close. Another first, eating breakfast with a man—wearing her robe and nightie no less! She felt vulnerable. Not that she was afraid of the man seated at the table, she was more afraid of her own unexpected reactions to him. And her own curiosity. She wanted to know more about him.

He shook his head in response.

Finishing the meal in silence, he pushed the plate away and leaned back in his chair, tilting it on its rear legs as he sighed. Coffee cup cradled against his chest, he smiled. "I think I'll make it until tonight. That was great, Jack. You should make French toast more often, you've got it down pat."

She smiled at his compliment, gathered from it that her sister wasn't much of a cook. But Julianne was. She had learned from her mother. "Glad you enjoyed it."

"Mmm, maybe I should make a habit of coming over more often for breakfast," he said, his eyes watchful.

She blinked, uncertain how to reply, tracing her finger along the rim of her coffee mug, heat engulfing her at the thought of his coming over for breakfast. What if she wore one of Jackie's sexy negligees the next time? Combed her hair before coming downstairs? Good grief, she'd just met the man and she already planned future breakfasts?

"How did you get in today?" she blurted.

"I used the key you gave me, how did you think?"

"Of course, the key." God, he had a key? Did Jackie have a key to his place?

"Get dressed, I'll meet you out on the beach in thirty minutes," he said as he drained his cup.

"Don't you have to go to work or something?" she asked, unsure she could pretend to be her sister all day with a neighbor who had known Jackie since she moved in. Wasn't it about two years ago? That she'd pulled it off so far seemed miraculous.

He shook his head. "What's the point of being president if I can't take a few days off? Besides, I'm too beat to be any good at the office. I'll probably nap on the beach but at least you'll be there to wake me up in your own inimitable style, right?"

His voice sent shivers along her spine, deep and husky and loaded with innuendos. She wondered what Jackie's "inimitable style" was. For a moment Julianne hesitated. This man fascinated her. He was nothing like the boys she'd dated in college, nothing like David. If he pursued a woman, he'd do it with panache and flare and make her feel more like a woman than anyone ever had. He would not bring bouquets of toothbrushes, or inundate her with flavored floss.

Guiltily, she looked away. David was honest in his feelings. She and he had been friends for years. It wasn't fair to mock him, even in her thoughts. She had to decide whether to marry him or not, and be ready to give her answer when she returned home. They would probably marry. David had always been safe and secure. There had been no great passion between them, he had never pushed for more than a few chaste kisses. But she knew him, could trust him to be a good husband and father. She just wished there was a bit more. Maybe it came with time.

He rose lazily and stretched. Lowering his arms, he moved smoothly around the table until he stood beside Julianne. Reaching down a finger, he tilted her face up to his. "Meet you in thirty minutes. Don't take all day."

"Right, thirty minutes." Time seemed to stand still as he gazed down into her eyes, his finger hot against her jaw.

She held her breath, imagining him leaning over until his lips touched hers, until the heat that rose in her met the heat he generated. Together they—

He playfully touched the tip of her nose with his finger and left.

Slowly Julianne let the air out of her lungs. Running her tongue over her lips, she imagined she could taste him. Would it be a curious blend of sweet syrup, strong coffee and sexy male? She shivered and jumped up. Running water in the sink, she gazed out over the wide expanse of ocean. Blood hummed in her veins, anticipation jumped up and down. Slowly she took a shaky breath and smiled. She wondered if she were losing her mind. She couldn't spend the entire day with this man. But a short time, maybe. For just a little while she'd pretend she was not the shy librarian from Charlottesville, but her carefree and daring, sophisticated sister.

Cade crossed the yard between the houses, puzzled with the events of the morning. Something was definitely different about his pretty neighbor. She hadn't acted a bit like herself— and it had nothing to do with coming down with a cold. But she could keep her secrets for the time being. He grinned. He had all day to find out what game she was playing. She'd once called him a hot-shot businessman, more interested in deals than the special effects he peddled. Maybe he'd demonstrate for the lady how he could use some of those business techniques to find out what she was up to.

And if that didn't work, he'd ply her with margaritas at dinner. She loved them and after only a few drinks became very loquacious. Shaking his head, he let himself back into his house. A good thing she didn't have to work. She'd never make it in business, she was usually totally predictable. Maybe that's why her actions this morning puzzled him. She seemed like a totally different woman.

Stepping beneath a hot shower a few minutes later, Cade continued worrying the puzzle Jackie presented. He'd known her for a couple of years, ever since she'd bought the house next door. Both of them were young, single, and comfortably established financially—he from his special effects, she from a rich ex-husband. As neighbors do, they'd exchanged pleasantries, gradually forming a kind of casual friendship. Enough to exchange keys, keep an eye on each other's place when one of them traveled. Enough to borrow coffee or milk from time to time.

They usually invited each other to parties they gave. Jackie proved to be a lot of fun and a knockout when she took the time and made the effort. But he'd made it clear in the beginning that his only interest was in neighborly friendship. Burned by his marriage and divorce, he'd sworn off women. At least, trying to trust one enough for marriage.

She said she felt the same, so they had slowly become friends of a sort.

For the most part he liked her, found her intriguing and occasionally sweet in a way that she tried to cover up. Not always, however. Not when she reminded him of his ex-wife, Crystal. Then, he wanted nothing to do with Jackie du Marcel, or any woman more concerned with having a good time than loyalty.

Twice over the past couple of years she'd asked him to listen to her reading for small parts in movies. When he suggested she should try for bigger roles, she had laughed merrily, shrugged and commented that the throwaway roles suited her. She did not want to put up with the grind of building a career.

Stepping from the shower, he dried off and wrapped the damp towel around his waist. Peering into the mirror, he considered shaving. Might as well, no sense looking as scruffy as a stray dog. He needed his hair cut and made a mental note to find time. Lathering his face, he paused in mid-swipe, staring at himself, still puzzled by the change in his neighbor. There had been something different—or at least, in his own mind.

For one thing he'd wanted to kiss her. He never wanted to get involved with another woman like Crystal, but he'd been tempted to carry out his invitation for a welcome home kiss. And he'd never felt so inclined before with Jackie. Must be jet lag.

He frowned. She had worn a terry-cloth robe and hadn't even combed her hair. Instead it had been tousled around her cheeks. Her eyes, wide and solemn, had intrigued him. Was that how she looked first thing each morning? He felt another stir of interest.

Maybe he should skip the beach and head straight for bed. The last thing he wanted was to imagine any attraction for his neighbor. They had developed a friendship that suited him perfectly. No sense getting sex mixed up in it.

Burned once years ago, Cade had no intentions of falling into that trap again. And especially not with a flighty, spend-thrift neighbor who craved attention wherever she went. Yet he couldn't explain the strange setup this morning—a terry-cloth bathrobe that covered her like a vestal virgin, a sultry voice with a hint of a Southern accent, and the delicious home-cooked breakfast from a woman who usually had difficulty boiling water. Was it an act? Which? The sophisticated di-vorcée or the vestal virgin?

Julianne cleaned the kitchen in less than five minutes. Hur-rying up to Jackie's room, she paused in the doorway. Where would her sister stash bathing suits? Julianne had worn her own suit yesterday, but curious to see the "crochet thingy," she wanted to find her sister's—if only to see what it looked like. Crossing to the huge dresser, Julianne began to open drawers. No bathing suits.

Entering the large walk-in closet, she pulled open the built-in drawers to the left.

"Bingo." The white tangle of yarn had to be the suit. Hold-ing it up, Julianne frowned. She had handkerchiefs that cov-ered more. Balling it up, she tossed it back into the drawer. No way would she wear something that revealing. It was her own or nothing.

She pulled on her one-piece dark blue suit, brushed her hair and reached for her sunscreen. Pausing as she caught a glimpse of herself in the huge wall of mirrors, she glanced at her re-flection. Her cheeks flushed in anticipation and excitement. Her eyes sparkled. For a moment she actually looked like her sister. It wasn't just features, those were identical. It was more attitude. This was without a doubt the wildest thing she'd ever done—and she felt so alive! Pure fantasy, she couldn't keep up this pretense for more than a little while. But if she could get through the morning, she'd have succeeded. For once in her life she planned to experience the adventures her sister took for granted.

No one would be hurt. As long as she kept it firmly in mind that this was only a fantasy, she couldn't be seduced into planning a life like Jackie's. When her vacation ended, she'd return to the library, to Charlottesville, and make up her mind about David. But that day was weeks away. For now she was free, on vacation and about to spend the day at the beach with the sexiest man she'd ever seen!

Snatching up a towel, sunglasses and a floppy hat, Julianne slid her feet into sandals and headed out.

Making her way down the stone steps carved into the cliff that rose above the crescent-shaped sandy strip of beach, she saw Cade Marshall already sitting on a colorful towel, watching the waves. Thank God, she'd remembered his name. Feeling confident with that bit of knowledge, she hurried down the rest of the steps and walked onto the cool white sand. Part of the small beach still lay in the shadow of the cliff. Even though early, the sun felt warm when she stepped out of the shade. The soft air blowing from the sea caressed her skin. She must have made a noise because Cade turned to watch her walk toward him.

"Less than a half hour," she said, suddenly shy as she felt his gaze on her. She should have worn a cover-up. Conscious of her long bare legs and the clinging suit, and his eyes scanning every inch of her, Julianne quickly spread her towel next to his and dropped to her knees. She had never felt like this before, nor had any man devoured her with his eyes. Flustered, her mind went blank as she stared into his incredible green gaze.

"That sunscreen?" he asked, gesturing to the tube in her hand.

"Yes, want some?" Reluctantly, she dragged her gaze to the container.

"Do my back." Cade turned and presented his tanned back.

Julianne swallowed. His shoulders were a yard wide, the muscles and taut tanned skin tempting her like nothing had done before. He wanted her to touch him? To spread lotion across that expanse, and keep her sanity? No, he'd said nothing about keeping her sanity. Fumbling with the cap, she finally got it off and poured some lotion into her palm. Taking a deep breath, she reached out to touch him.

"Jack, did you fall asleep?" he grumbled.

"Hold your horses." She slapped the lotion onto the middle of his back.

He tightened up and pulled away. "Hey, that's cold!"

She caught her bottom lip with her teeth to keep a telltale giggle from escaping. Slowly she reached out and spread the lotion, soothing it over the sculpted muscles, following the slight indentation of his spine. Her fingertips tingled with his heat as she smoothed and kneaded the taut skin. Up and down, side to side, mesmerized by the shimmering waves of sensation that rushed from her hand to her heart and to every cell in her body. Thinking about what Jackie had said about ringing chimes, Julianne knew Cade Marshall could ring an entire carillon, probably without even trying.

"Jack," he said, his voice hard to hear over the surf.

"What?" Every inch of his back was slathered in white sunscreen, but still she couldn't stop touching him. Sleek and toned and hard. She wondered how he stayed so fit if he worked with computers. Didn't programmers spend hours hunched over a keyboard? His skin should have been pasty white instead of deeply tanned. His eyes should squint instead of looking so open and expressive.

"Did something happen while I was gone?" he asked.

"Like what?" Reluctantly, she dropped her hand and smoothed the excess lotion onto the tops of her thighs.

Cade turned to face her. "I don't know. Did you have a falling out with a guy? Pass a milestone birthday? Go bankrupt? You tell me."

He suspected. How long before he realized she wasn't Jackie? Dare she admit it? Opening her mouth to do just that, Julianne snapped it shut, concentrating on rubbing in the sunscreen. Just for today, would it hurt to pretend? If he discovered her deception, he'd probably be so disgusted he'd storm off and never speak to her again. Could it hurt just for one day?

Raising her lashes until she could look at him, she shook her head. "Nothing happened. My birthday is in October."

"Something's up, Jack. If I weren't so damned tired, I'd probably be able to figure it out. You are not acting like you normally do. If it's something to do with us, I think you'd better spit it out."

"There's nothing."

He looked at her and shook his head. "First, you were not in a cranky mood when I woke you up hours earlier than you like to get up. Next, I never saw a plainer robe than the one you wore this morning. Where was that see-through thing you shocked me with that time I came over unexpectedly? Next thing I know, you're playing Little Miss Domestic and fixing me breakfast, which was delicious, by the way. Now the virtuous swimsuit, not the crocheted one you like to wear. That all adds up to something fishy, in my book."

He hadn't moved, but Julianne felt cornered. She inched back, frantically scrambling around for something to say to disarm his suspicions. Maybe she should just tell him who she was and why she was pretending to be her sister. Licking her dry lips, she stalled, hoping something clever would pop into her mind. She didn't want to admit it yet. She enjoyed having the man interested in her, thinking she was Jackie. It was novel

and exciting and she wanted to share this time and space with
Cade Marshall.

"You know how I feel about honesty. There's nothing more
important. I'd rather know right up front if something's going
on."

"Have we had this conversation before?" she asked. *Honesty?* She didn't know precisely how he felt, but she had a
good idea after that remark. All the more reason to delay confessing her masquerade, or avoid confessing at all. She'd see
if she could pull it off today, then avoid him like the plague.
If luck was on her side, she could fool him for the few hours
they spent on the beach. She'd come up with an excuse to
skip dinner.

"About honesty? You know we have. I've made no secret
about what I think about lying and deceiving people. A hang-
up from Crystal."

Julianne considered her options. She could hide in the house
until Jackie returned. Or take the flashy car from the garage
and drive until she ran out of gas. Or return home tomorrow
after the mortifying exposure of her deception.

Or continue the bluff.

Cade rubbed his eyes with his thumb and forefinger. "I'm
so tired I can hardly think."

"You should sleep," she said gently, relieved by the change
of subject.

"Don't want to, I can get back on California time better if
I stay up today and sleep tonight."

"From the looks of you, if you don't take at least a nap
today, you'll fall asleep in the middle of dinner," she said,
exasperated.

He shook his head. "You're right, I won't last that long."
Stretching out on his towel, his long legs pushed into the sand.
"Don't let me sleep long enough to get burned," he mumbled,
pillowing his head on his stacked hands.

In two seconds Julianne heard the deep breathing. He'd
fallen asleep.

Life in the fast lane, she thought wryly. She proved so exciting, she put her companion to sleep before they'd been on the beach for ten minutes.

Cade awoke still feeling exhausted. His internal clock kept him from sleeping soundly. Time enough for that later when he'd sleep the night through. Opening his eyes a slit, he stared at Jackie. She sat beside him, watching the surf. Turning his wrist slightly, he saw he'd been asleep for more than forty-five minutes. He was surprised she had hung around. As long as he'd known her, she had been too restless to sit still for any length of time. Always on the go, always wanting fun and people and action, it seemed unlike her to sit quietly on the beach while he slept.

Another inconsistency to ponder. Once he caught up on his rest, he'd figure it out. For now he liked looking at her. In the sun, the highlights in her hair shone almost gold. He'd always though of her hair as just light brown, but the streaks of brightness added an intriguing aura. Her profile was perfect, with the wisp of bangs on her forehead teasing his fingers to brush them away. She seemed paler than when he'd last seen her, but the golden sheen to her skin drew his eye, as did the sleek one-piece bathing suit. While far from old-fashioned, it nevertheless covered more of her than normal. Yet he found it alluring.

Alluring? Hell, this was Jackie, the next-door neighbor he borrowed coffee from, not some woman to get involved with.

Yet he could swear there was something different about her, something that caught his attention. Attracted to her? He didn't like the idea. When he'd first met her, he'd felt nothing. Over the past couple of years, nothing. Why today? It had to be the jet lag. It had to be because he was so damn tired. It seemed as if he were seeing her for the first time, seeing how drop-dead gorgeous she looked. And seeing a different side to her.

She licked her lips, her pink tongue darting out for a second. Desire gripped him. Shocked him. He couldn't believe he had the hots for his neighbor! He didn't like glamour women. Crystal had taught her lesson well, and shattered any illusions he might have held. But for the first time he really saw Jackie as a beautiful woman. And there was something different about her, something softer, almost sweeter.

She turned, saw he was awake and smiled. Cade held still, amazed at the lust that swamped him. *He wanted her.* Here and now. In his bed, her bed, later. It didn't matter, he wanted Jacqueline du Marcel!

"Did that take off the edge?" she asked, her eyes bright with an innocence that surprised him.

"It'll do." Stunned at his reaction, at his body's response to the woman beside him, he pushed himself up and turned quickly toward the ocean. With the abbreviated bathing suit he wore, his lusty feelings would be clear for the world to see in about two seconds. A cool swim was in order.

"A quick dip will help me shake the dregs." Walking away before she could scramble to her feet, he plunged into the waves, swimming beyond the surf and into the deeper water. It wasn't cold enough.

Jackie followed and in seconds swam up beside him, keeping pace.

"Wow, this is much colder than I expected. Not at all like Virginia Beach," she said, swimming in wide circles around him when he began to tread water.

"When were you in Virginia Beach?" he asked, kicking lazily. Her hair was plastered to her head, droplets sparkled from her lashes. He wanted to taste the salt on her lips, the sweetness behind them. Meeting her gaze, he went on alert. She looked as guilty as a child caught stealing cookies.

"One time a while back." She moved away, Cade followed.

"Tell me about it, you never mentioned it before." He easily caught up, kept pace.

"The water there is much warmer. This water's cold."

"I'm surprised you came in. Usually you don't."

"I was getting hot on the sand."

She was obviously flustered. Why? Eyes narrowed, he moved closer, bumping into her, catching her when she would pull away. Holding her, his legs kicked enough to keep them upright, riding the swells that moved beneath them. They drifted south, but still had plenty of beach left.

She pushed against him. "Let me go, please."

"Afraid I'll dunk you?" he teased. He didn't want to dunk her beneath the water, he wanted to pull her into his arms and kiss her.

"You and what three other guys?" In two seconds she had slipped from his grasp beneath the water and moved several feet away. Coming up for air, she laughed.

"Race you back to the shore," he challenged, just to see what she'd do. He grew more perplexed by her behavior every moment they were together.

"Done!" She propelled herself toward the beach, swimming as hard as she could. He gave her five seconds and took off after her. It was a mistake. She beat him to the beach by inches.

"I win!" Laughing, she sloshed through the foaming surf and gained the firm-packed beach. Skimming her hands over her hair, she gazed up at the clear blue sky, her joy in the day expressed for all to see.

"So you get the prize," he said, following her from the water.

"What is it?" Wringing out her hair, she fluffed the damp strands with her fingertips.

"This." He pulled her against him and lowered his mouth to hers. Her lips were cool and tasted of salt. He wanted more than a brush of lips. Would she reciprocate? Slowly he felt her mouth move against his, open to the gentle pressure of his tongue against the seam of her mouth. Slipping inside, he felt the heat, tasted her unique flavor, the contrast to the sea salt both exotic and sweet. He wanted more. Slowly pulling her cool body against his, he felt his own skin heat, then warm hers. Softness met hardness, passion met rising passion as he deepened the kiss and glided one hand over her back, from her shoulders to the gentle swell of her hips.

Her body moved against his in tantalizing temptation. Her mouth responded, shyly at first. He found the uncertainty erotic, intoxicating him, building his need and desire to monumental proportions. He'd known the woman for more than two years but the raw need that filled him at this moment staggered him. He had never felt like this before.

When she pushed against him, he eased his tight hold, pulling back enough to gaze into her stunned eyes.

Taking a trembling breath, she asked, "And what would your prize have been if you'd won?"

"This." He kissed her again, as hard, as long. And drew the same response as before. When he pulled back this time, both of them were breathing hard.

She licked her lips, her tongue taking its sweet time. Cade groaned, pulling her closer.

"No. Stop. This is a public beach, Cade!"

"I knew it! You're up to something, Jackie. When did you let something as inconsequential as being on a public beach stop you? What are you playing at? You've never come close enough for me to touch, much less kiss before. What is going on?"

"Excuse me. I don't think I was the one kissing. If anything, I was the kissee."

"As soon as I get enough sleep that I can think straight, I'll figure it out, so you might as well tell me what's going on," he said a bit roughly.

Julianne pushed away, and headed back toward their towels. He'd probably figure it out in two minutes if he wasn't almost dead from jet lag. And when he did, how would she explain why she'd lied? Why she'd pretended she was Jackie? What a mess. To save herself a flood of embarrassment, she ought to leave instantly.

"Jackie?"

"You're tired. We were playing in the water and what else could you offer as a prize?" she rationalized.

The sun now rode high in the sky; the warm air dried her skin; the sand grew hot beneath her feet. Yesterday she'd brought the umbrella, but she'd left it in the shed this morning. Maybe she should get it. She didn't want to burn, there was too much yet to do on her vacation to be incapacitated by sunburn. She could use that as an excuse to escape. Come back to the beach after he went home.

"Give me your lotion, I'll spread it on your back." Cade came up beside her, silently. She jumped and shook her head. There was no way she could think with him touching her, his kisses had proved that. She licked her lips, tasted him on them and felt heat blossom deep within.

They were on a public beach, for heaven's sake, and she'd almost forgotten that. Actually she'd almost forgotten her name. His kisses had blown a fuse and she needed to get some sort of control over her rampant emotions. Longing went deep. Desire flooded each cell. Need clamored for release.

Sitting on her towel, she rubbed lotion on her skin, her neck and shoulders, each arm, and her legs. Replacing the cap, she lay back and closed her eyes. Even behind her closed eyelids the imprint of Cade standing beside her remained sharp and clear.

"If you had worn your bikini, you could remove the top so not to have lines," he said lazily. From the direction of his voice, he had apparently sat on his towel.

"Oh, like I'm going topless here," she muttered, shocked at the suggestion.

"Why not? It's not as if you haven't done it before, or was that story about the French Riviera just an exaggeration?"

"This isn't the south of France."

"No, but it's just you and me." Humor laced his tone.

She opened her eyes, squinting in the sun's glare, and tried to frown at him. "Don't you have somewhere else to be?"

He chuckled and leaned over her. She squirmed away and closed her eyes.

She heard him move, yet his fingers on her jaw were unexpected as he tilted her head in his direction. She opened her eyes a slit. His head blocked the sun.

"I wasn't the only one in that kiss. I felt your response. You can't hide something like that." Blunt and bold, he stated the fact and nothing more.

Her heart caught, raced. Blood pounded through her. Fire licked through her veins. The sun might burn her skin, but his words melted her center. For one blinding moment she wondered what it would be like to make love with Cade Marshall. His kisses almost shattered her, making love would probably finish the job. But what a glorious way to go.

Then reality set in. He thought she was Jackie. He didn't even know her.

The reality was staggering. Appealing, exciting, daring. No one had ever found her captivating enough to kiss her as passionately as he'd done. Her heart pounded so hard it shook her body. The delightful images that flooded her mind almost melted her resistance. Would he kiss her again? Push for a closer relationship? Want to make love with her?

Good grief, she had just met the man! She was not a woman to give in to hot passionate affairs with strangers. She and the man who had proposed to her had never made love. What was she thinking?

That was the problem, she wasn't thinking. When around Cade Marshall, she discovered she couldn't think at all. Just feel. And the feelings were outside her normal realm.

But vacation or not, there were limits!

Three

Julianne caught her breath as every nerve ending stood at attention. Swallowing hard, she pushed his hand away and sat up. He leaned too close. She scrambled to her knees, determined not to flee, but unsure she could stay and talk to him. Her thoughts were in turmoil, contradictory feelings surged through her. His green eyes blazed as he stared at her, waiting, watching.

"You're too close," she blurted, then wanted to wrap the towel over her head. The last word in sophistication? No, she sounded like the frightened teenager.

He shrugged and leaned on one elbow, his gaze never leaving hers, the frown of puzzlement giving way to speculation. "I'm not touching you. How close is close?"

She looked out at the blue water, feeling as foolish as she must look. She led a quiet life in a college town, not some wild party existence like Jackie. But he thought she did. She was not the type to casually kiss men, he'd see that in no time.

Yet, why not? Hadn't her sister said they were more alike

than Julianne realized, after all, they were twins. If he thought Jackie would be willing to kiss a bit, why not her?

Jackie! What would this do to her sister and her relationship with her neighbor? Obviously this needed much more thought. Though she found it impossible to think when Cade sat close enough that she could feel his heat, or when his eyes stared into hers like green lasers searching, searching. Or when his breath fanned across her cheeks.

"What did you think we'd do, Jack? Run amok after one or two kisses and end up in a bedroom? Give me a little credit for a bit of finesse."

Warmth spread across her chest, up her neck and into her cheeks. Tilting her head slightly as she gravely stared at him, she almost nodded. Without thinking, she reached out and ran her fingertips along his shoulders. He felt hot and sleek and so sexy Julianne knew she was way out of her league. The question was, could she survive a few kisses and not fall into a summer fling?

When he took her hand and kissed each fingertip, Julianne knew it didn't matter if she survived or not, she wanted this. But she couldn't go against twenty-four years of living.

Snatching back her hand, she smiled shakily. "Do you still want to tell me about your trip to Italy? I'd love to hear more about your work, how you got started…" She trailed off, worried he'd already covered this with Jackie.

He reached for her hand, holding it firmly in his, drawing it up until his lips brushed across her wrist, sending waves of tingling awareness up her arm. His smile caught her eyes and she couldn't look away. Wishing she felt comfortable enough to lean forward slightly and touch her lips to the bare skin of his shoulder, she left her hand in his, tightening her grip slightly. Now what? Did she look as inept and scared as she felt?

"I'll tell you all about Italy, and then we can compare notes with what you saw when you visited Rome and Florence. We can swim again if you like, or just laze around on the beach for a while. I have to go up to the house sometime this afternoon and check in with the office, but the rest of the day is free.''

She nodded, watching him warily, slowly relaxing. He didn't seem mad she'd refused to play his game. His voice sounded calm, matter-of-fact. A twinge of disappointment stabbed. She would have liked a bit more. If he had really wanted to kiss her again, wouldn't he have pushed harder?

''Then we'll go to Garcia's and—''

Her heart pounded as she thought about trying to continue the bluff through dinner.

''—Hope I can stay awake long enough to eat,'' Cade said. He lay back on the towel, and slowly opened his hand.

She withdrew hers and scooted a bit farther away, as if that would dampen the uncertainty that plagued her. Maybe it wouldn't, but a bit of distance would let her garner some semblance of control. She had a feeling she'd remember this day all her life!

They lay side by side in the sun, dozing, turning. Cade asked her to reapply the sunscreen. Julianne complied, wondering if this could be considered a form of foreplay. When she rubbed his back, she took her time, savoring each stroke of her palm against the hard muscles that bunched and relaxed beneath her touch. She'd never had such luxury of exploring a man's body before, never experienced the sensuous awareness so much touching brought.

When she turned onto her stomach, Cade returned the favor, slipping down the straps of her suit, teasing her by easing his fingertips beneath the edge of the spandex and coating skin that would never see the sunlight. Her eyes tightly closed, she tried to breathe normally. She felt as if she were on fire, but refrained from protesting, savoring the sensations long after he lay back down and dozed off.

Julianne turned her head and studied the man, from the tousled dark hair to the firm jut of his jaw. His bathing suit was skimpier than those worn by most men she knew, fitting like a glove. Hiding nothing.

Her cheeks grew warm as she stared, imagining what would happen if she had not pulled away from his electrifying kisses. She couldn't see herself in a role of femme fatale, but her imagination proved wondrous. Closing her eyes, she could feel his hands on her back, the long, languorous strokes designed to soothe and inflame. With little effort he could have turned her onto her back and continued slipping beneath the edge of her suit, stroking...her eyes flew open.

Before she could give in to temptation, she jumped to her feet and headed for the cool water, yanking up the straps to her suit, giving herself a firm talking-to. She swam slowly, feeling the brisk sea cool her overheated body. Now if it would cool her overactive imagination, she might make it through the day!

"Cooling off?" Cade asked a few minutes later, joining her beyond the breakers.

Julianne swirled around and met his knowing eyes. She shrugged, trying to appear nonchalant. "The sun's getting hot."

"It's not the only thing getting hot." He swam close, treading water. His legs tangled with hers beneath the surface.

"Cade," she said, feeling shy at the glint in his eyes.

"I know, I've been shot down. I won't press, cupcake."

"Cupcake?"

He shrugged and splashed her with water. "You taste as sweet as a cupcake. I never knew that before. See what a man can learn from a kiss."

Shyness bloomed. Tongue-tied, she sought for something to say, wishing deep in her heart that he would press, that he would persevere. "I'm getting hungry. Want to come up to the house for lunch?"

"Did someone do some kind of transplant on you while I was gone? First breakfast, now you want to fix lunch? This isn't some kind of nesting instinct, is it?'' he asked suspiciously.

"Slapping something together between two pieces of bread is hardly cordon bleu cooking, Cade. If you're worried, I'll make it peanut butter and jelly.''

He chuckled, staying close, running his hand down her arm and tangling his fingers with hers. Drawing their linked hand up, he kissed her fingers. "I'm willing to bet you don't even have PB&J in your house. But I'm not one to say no to a free meal.''

"Second one today,'' she reminded him sassily.

"So I'll treat dinner. Let's go, it's got to be close to noon and I'm hungry. Besides, I'll need the energy to keep going this afternoon.'' He released her hand as they swam leisurely toward the shore.

"You should take a nap,'' she said.

"I've had two this morning.''

"Not long ones. If you end facedown in the guacamole, don't look to me to clean it off,'' she teased, amazed at her own boldness. Of course he didn't realize they'd just met. Was this how her sister lived? It was fun!

"I'll remember that.''

"Want to race back?'' she asked, maneuvering herself closer to the beach.

"Sure, but no handicap this time.''

Cade reached the sand first and waited to walk out of the water with Julianne.

"Now I get the prize,'' he said, and kissed her. Julianne almost sank to her knees when he released her. Ignoring the glint in his eyes, she forced her knees to work as she hurried to the towels. Shakily, she gathered her things and turned to follow him up the rock steps cut into the bluff. Her blood tingled. There was no other word to describe the sensation. All thoughts of avoiding him in the future fled. Uncertainty aside, she liked the way she felt around him.

"I'll shower and change and be right over. Keep the peanut

butter warm," he said when they reached the top. Touching her lightly on her nose, he headed for home.

Julianne watched as he walked along the path between the cliff and the back of his sprawling stucco house. She was in big trouble. Never in her life had she become so fascinated, so captivated, by anyone. Watching him walk away, she felt suddenly alone, bereft. For a moment she toyed with the idea of following him, waiting at his house while he showered.

Instant infatuation—and at her age.

Julianne trudged up the path to her sister's house. Cade would be over in a few minutes and her bubbling senses would again boil over. Was this how Jackie had felt around Jean? No wonder she'd said he rang her chimes.

Showered, dressed in her own white shorts and a light blue tank top, Julianne headed for the kitchen to begin to make the sandwiches. Being in the fresh air and sunshine had given her a huge appetite. She suspected Cade would be equally hungry. Would he tease her again, or be too tired to do much more than eat? Glancing at the clock, she wondered when he'd arrive. She looked out the window at the yard; no sign of him yet. Impatiently she sliced part of the roast they'd bought at the deli section of the supermarket.

The phone rang. It was Cade.

"Hi, babe. I can't make lunch, after all. There were a dozen phone messages waiting for me about another problem that cropped up with the Italian deal. I have to go into the office this afternoon."

"Oh." Disappointment swamped her. She leaned dejectedly against the wall. "I understand." She might understand, but she didn't like it.

"Dinner's still on. I'll pick you up around seven. That suit you?"

"Yes, seven's fine. I'll be ready."

"Jackie?" He stopped.

"What?" Julianne's heart raced. She wished he'd invite her

to go in with him, spend the rest of the day together as they'd planned.

"Nothing. See you at seven."

Hanging up the phone, Julianne looked at the bread already spread with mayonnaise and the cold cuts she'd put out. Taking a slice of cheddar, she nibbled as she began to rewrap everything. It was a long time until seven.

When the phone rang a couple of minutes later, her spirits soared. Maybe he'd changed his mind.

"Hello?"

"Hello, darling. How was your trip?"

"Hi, Mom. I guess I should have called." Three days in California and her family seemed light-years away. She dragged a chair nearer to the phone and sat, annoyed at the disappointed she felt that it wasn't Cade. She loved her family and was glad to hear from her mother.

"Oh, no, Julianne, I love fretting for days on end, imagining you kidnapped or worse."

She laughed. "Mom, I flew directly here from Dulles, not much chance of getting kidnapped. And it's not like we have millions to pay a ransom."

"How's your sister?" Peggy Hamilton moved on to the next topic, her point made.

"Fine. Actually she's not here right now. She's in another movie and had to go to the filming early."

"That's a shame. Will she be back soon?"

"So she said. Just a week."

"Oh, honey, I'm sorry your vacation is ruined. Maybe instead of sitting around all alone in a strange place, you should come home and visit Jackie another time."

"Um, I'm not exactly alone. I mean, I am alone right now, but her neighbor and I are going out to dinner tonight. And Jackie's house is right on the beach. I went swimming yesterday and this morning."

"That's nice. If her neighbor takes you under her wing,

you'll get to see something of California while waiting for your sister's return.''

Julianne twisted the phone cord in her fingers. "The neighbor is a he, Mom," she said slowly. Maybe she should have just kept her mouth shut, let her mother think a woman was her new friend.

"David stopped by yesterday. He told us he'd asked you to marry him," Peggy said slowly.

Yes, she should have kept quiet, Julianne thought, grimacing. Now her mother would give her the why-didn't-you-tell-me routine.

"Yes, he did." Julianne frowned, wondering why he had stopped by her parents' place. Just to make sure they knew of his proposal? She wouldn't put it past him to try to get them on his side, added pressure to get his own way. Was this the first time she'd noticed how he plotted to get his own way more times than not?

"I must admit to being a bit surprised you didn't mention it. David's a nice boy," her mother said gently.

"He's four years older than I am, hardly a boy." Except when compared to Cade Marshall. Disliking the trend of her thoughts, she spoke again. "I'm very fond of David. But I told him I needed to think it over. After all, marriage is a big step. I want to make sure I know what I'm doing."

Julianne heard the sigh across the lines.

"Honey, if you have to think it over, that ought to give you a hint of what your answer should be. I had no hesitation when Gerald asked me."

"How about when Dad asked?"

"None there, either. But I think the relationship I've built with Gerald is far more substantial than what I had with your father," Peggy said dryly. "You know we've been happily married for sixteen years."

"And what you and Gerald have is what I want. David is sweet and dependable like Gerald."

"Yes he is, and has a good solid profession that would

always provide a steady income, also like Gerald. With your father it was always feast or famine. Of course, lately I understand it's been a steady feast, for which I'm glad for him. It's your decision, honey. I could mention Stacey was with him when he stopped by.''

"Stacey? His hygienist?" Julianne asked, puzzled. She'd seen Stacey many times when she'd stopped by for David. The woman worked two days a week. Plump and shy, she'd scarcely said four words to Julianne in the years she'd known her.

"She just got back from a vacation and looks stunning.''

"Stacey?''

"Apparently she spent her vacation at some health farm and lost a ton of weight, got her hair cut, new clothes. She looked really pretty yesterday.''

"Mom, I'm detecting a drift to this conversation. If I think I'm going to accept David's proposal, I'd better get home and defend my man, right?''

Peggy laughed. "No, if he wants to marry you, he'll still want that no matter how many beautiful women come through his office. I'm just catching you up on the news.''

"Right. How are Gerald and the kids?''

"The boys are up to their tricks again. Kari is going to spend the night this weekend at a slumber party at Marybeth's. And you know your brothers, they are threatening to show up and wreak havoc. I think Gerald's planning to take them camping. I'd have a night to myself.''

"Sounds great. Give everyone my love. I'll be home before long.''

"Enjoy your stay there, darling. And give Jackie my love. Tell her we wish she'd come to visit.''

"Mom, she knows that.''

"Then why doesn't she come?''

"I don't know. I'll work on it. 'Bye.''

Julianne hung up the phone, a feeling of homesickness sweeping her. Three days gone from home and she missed her family. Life in California might prove more exciting, but it was only temporary. She couldn't imagine living alone like Jackie relying on letters and phone calls to keep in touch. Not seeing their mother for years on end, not being a part of her brothers' and sister's lives. It seemed a bit lonely to Julianne.

Maybe life in the fast lane wasn't the perfect existence. There was a lot to be said for home and family and love.

Julianne called Garcia's during the afternoon and talked to the hostess. Having a good idea of appropriate dress, she scanned the colorful array in her sister's closet. Choosing a bright turquoise dress, she found strappy high heels that went with it. She took her time getting ready, anticipation and trepidation warring within as she thought about the night ahead.

Refusing to continue kissing on the beach was one thing, she thought as she wiped away the smear from her mascara with nervous hands, but the truth of the matter was, she couldn't forget the kiss. His words hovered in the air between them. She had participated. Had wanted more, though she couldn't admit that to Cade!

And it wasn't as if he wanted *her,* Julianne Bennet. Cade thought he was attracted to her sister. How would he feel if he discovered she'd tricked him? He'd already commented about disliking liars. She studied her face in the large mirror.

She ought to tell him. Tonight, before things went any further.

They'd already gone too far. He'd be angry, but she hadn't crossed any major lines. And it wasn't as if she ever had to see him again. She could take a drive up the coast, go to Disneyland or down to Mexico until Jackie returned home.

Taking a deep breath, she tried to calm her roiling nerves. She wanted this one day. Wanted to see what it was like to be carefree and sought after. She'd keep her distance and not allow any more kisses. Tomorrow, she'd make sure she stayed busy and avoided her sister's sexy neighbor.

First, dinner. For a few more hours she'd enjoy the fantasy, then when he brought her home, she'd say goodbye and that would end it. She wasn't out to harm anyone, she only wanted to taste a bit of the life-style her sister enjoyed.

Cade turned into the circle drive in front of Jackie's house, his black Porsche gleaming in the late afternoon sun. His love for his car made the drive into Hollywood bearable each day. Rubbing his eyes, he stopped and started to get out when he heard Jackie close her front door. Staring, he smiled when she waved and hurried to the car. He reached across the seat and opened the door, wondering for the tenth time what game she played.

If he didn't know her, hadn't known her for a couple of years, he'd swear she was not Jackie du Marcel. Too many things added up to almost a different person. Of course she was Jackie, wearing that blue-green dress he'd seen before. The loose top revealed creamy shoulders. The flared skirt danced as she walked, displaying her shapely legs. He liked looking at her.

Tonight, there were further discrepancies to the woman he thought he knew. He was surprised to see her sling a purse the size of an attaché case over her shoulder. In the past Jackie had seemed totally unencumbered by a purse. When she'd come to his last party, she'd put her key in her shoe.

In fact, that afternoon at the office, he'd mentioned being thrown by the differences. There was a kind of sweetness about his neighbor he'd never noticed before. The hard edge he was used to was missing. She'd appeared almost *shy* when they'd shared breakfast. If he didn't know better, he'd think she were some fresh young innocent, instead of a worldly divorcée. Yet there had been something oddly appealing about Jackie that morning. That fact alone kept her in the forefront of his thoughts. Marc, one of his resident techies, had suggested alien abduction as an explanation for the changes in Jackie. But then, Marc was into "Star Trek" and "The X-Files." Cade's secretary, Helen, had suggested amnesia, but he'd seen no signs of that. Yet, not once had Jackie made reference to anything in their shared past. And did she normally eschew that silky dressing gown for a terry-cloth one?

"Did you get the problem solved?" she asked, pulling the door shut and reaching for her seat belt.

"For the most part. Pete's still in Italy and needed some help from this end. I think he can manage the rest. I'll have to go into work early in the morning to make sure it's fixed."

She turned to smile at him and Cade felt a kick low in the gut. For the moment he didn't care what game she played. She looked beautiful; her eyes sparkled, her hair swirled around her, kissing her cheeks, and the blue-green of her dress made her skin glow. He wanted her. He'd known her for two years yet the primal urge to mate with this woman had emerged only today. Leaning over, he breathed in the fresh sultry scent that he recognized from that morning. A new perfume? Making a show of checking her seat belt to cover his actions, he sat back and put the car in gear. Great, he acted like a hormone-raging teenager.

"I missed you this afternoon. I took a book to read, sat beneath an umbrella on the beach."

He headed toward the restaurant. Another inconsistency—he'd never heard Jackie admitted to missing anyone. Of course he didn't spend much time with her.

"I could have found much more interesting things to do than work through a software glitch this afternoon," he agreed. "We could have spent the rest of the day together."

"Yes." She pleated the skirt of her dress nervously. Cade reached over and took her hand, linking their fingers, resting them on his thigh. Flicking her a glance, he almost smiled. She looked shocked. Her gaze drifted to their hands. The feel of her soft palm against his notched up his interest. If he felt this way after a good night's sleep, he'd do something about it. She was the jaded world traveler, maybe she wanted to be chased. Maybe he should have pushed her more, not accepted her refusal so easily.

But he still couldn't believe he had this overwhelming desire for his neighbor.

Cade drove competently through the winding canyon roads until he reached the flatlands. The parking lot at Garcia's was crowded, as usual, but he found a place along the outer rim.

"Don't want to get a ding, huh?" she teased as he opened her door. They had the length of the parking lot to walk.

"Not on this baby."

Garcia's was housed in an old adobe structure with a wide courtyard surrounded by a low stucco wall. Couples gathered around the small tables in the courtyard, sipping margaritas and enjoying the mariachi band playing softly in the corner. Festive lanterns illuminated the patio and the warm Southern California evening made the setting perfect.

"Drinks first?" Cade asked as they waited for the hostess.

"Sounds good."

They were seated at one of the small patio tables, a flickering candle in the center. The evening air was balmy and still. Gentle laughter, the murmur of voices and the Spanish music gave the setting a certain charm Julianne had never seen.

"Margarita?" Cade asked.

"I'll just have white wine," Julianne said, looking around with avid interest.

"The last time we were here you insisted there was nothing else to drink at a Mexican restaurant but margaritas," he mentioned casually, leaning back in his chair, stretching his legs beneath the table. His calf brushed against hers.

"I did?" Julianne said, swallowing hard, resisting the urge to shift her leg away. Suddenly she felt as if the two of them were alone in a soft Southern night. "I'd like wine tonight," she said, stalling. "This is nice." She forced her gaze elsewhere.

"You said once it was your favorite restaurant. Going to have the usual when we order?"

She blinked. "I don't know. I'll check out the menu first.

Maybe I'll try something new tonight.'' She cleared her throat nervously, unsettled by the watchful—suspicious?—look in Cade's gaze.

When the drinks arrived, he picked up his beer and touched the rim to her wineglass.

''To kisses on the beach,'' he said softly.

Her gaze met his and held. Slowly she nodded and took a sip, unable to say a word. Her throat felt tight, butterflies of shyness filled her.

When Cade reached for her hand, she made no protest. He glanced down, as if intrigued by the contrast of his larger tanned hand holding her pale one. She liked his touch. She wanted to have him touch her all over, feel his fingers against her skin, his palms against her body. Discover if the tingling pleasure that shot up her arm would explode into even more powerful reactions if he explored her intimately.

Heat blossomed. She sipped the wine in an attempt to cool down.

''Scoot your chair closer, it's hard to hold a conversation with so many people around,'' he ordered gently.

She complied instantly, until her legs brushed against his, until her shoulder almost touched his. She had never felt so desirable, so desired. *Or so scared.* What was she doing playing games with this man?

''What do you want to talk about?'' she asked, tilting her head until her lips were perfectly aligned for his. Flirting with danger, recklessly daring to push the limits, she lightly touched the tip of her tongue along her top lip, her gaze locked with his. The blood pounding through her veins drowned out the noise from the other diners.

Leaning forward, he kissed her quickly, lightly, uttering a soft groan as his lips caressed hers.

Julianne kept her eyes open, mesmerized by the gleam in his. When he leaned back, she released her breath, unaware she'd been holding it. A kiss couldn't hurt. But it could short-circuit her senses. She wanted more. This wasn't the first time she wished she were a more damn-the-consequences person.

"Do you remember that party you had a few months ago, when we ended up on your patio talking about family and friends and tropical settings we'd visited?"

"Party?" His thoughts jumped around so much. She was still recovering from his kiss.

He frowned. "You couldn't have forgotten, you gave it."

"I...no, of course, I didn't forget." She cleared her throat. "It's been a while, what about it?"

"If your memory is fading that fast, you'll have a hell of a time when you're eighty."

Eighty? If she didn't stop this masquerade soon, the stress would make sure she didn't live through tomorrow, no need to worry about making eighty.

She took a sip of wine. "What about the party?"

"We got sidetracked before we could complete our life histories. Tell me more about yours. We've been neighbors for two years, but I don't know that much about you. Tell me about your family."

"My family?" He wanted to know about her family? What had Jackie told him? That she had a twin? That she had a sister who never came to visit, but kept in touch through long letters while Jackie rarely dashed off more than a sentence or two, relying on phone calls to keep in touch?

"Family—you know, mother, father, siblings. I know more than I need to about your father, the tabloids and fan magazines keep everyone up to date with the Hollywood crowd. You told me once he divorced your mother ages ago. How about the rest of your family? Do you have any brothers or sisters?"

"Brothers or sisters?"

He leaned back. "Yes, brothers or sisters. Is it too noisy here? Should we go somewhere else?"

"No, this is fine. Yes, I have."

"What?"

"Brothers and sisters. To be accurate, I have two half-brothers and a half-sister. My mother remarried after she and my father split." If she had much more wine, she'd be sloshed before dinner, Julianne thought, taking another sip to stall, to give herself time to think.

"What about—"

"Sir, I have a table for you." The waitress stopped by the table, a wide smile on her face.

Cade nodded and stood, stepping aside for Julianne.

She rose, grateful for the interruption. In her effort to escape the inquisition, she swung around the table, giving Cade a wide berth. Unfortunately, her purse caught on the edge of a chair, tipped, and dumped its entire contents on the tiled patio. Brush, lipstick, change purse—and a dozen sample sizes of flavored dental floss.

Four

Cade stooped and began to gather the small plastic boxes, reading the labels. Peppermint, cherry, root beer. *Root beer?* He looked up, arrested by the sight of Jackie scrambling around gathering up spilled items. She avoided his eyes as she stuffed comb, lipstick, wallet back into the large handbag.

She held out her hand and Cade slowly stood up, dropping the dental floss onto her palm.

"Floss?" he asked. Was his brain on a total hiatus? Was he imagining things? Glamorous world traveler Jackie du Marcel carrying around a bagful of dental floss?

She turned and followed the waitress, her head held high. But the sway of her hips caught his attention. Rubbing his hands across his burning eyes, he followed, feeling as if he were caught up in "The Twilight Zone."

When they'd been seated and a second round of drinks ordered, he ignored the large menu and stared across the booth at Jackie who appeared to be trying to hide behind the colorful listing of tonight's specials.

"Jackie, why do you have a dozen or more containers of flavored dental floss in your purse?" he asked.

She peered at him over the edge of the menu. "Do you think I don't floss?" she asked.

He shrugged. "To tell the truth, I never gave it any thought. But flavored floss? And so many of them?"

"I got them from my dentist—to try. He gives those little boxes away to his patients and wanted my opinion on the flavored ones." She ducked behind the menu again.

Cade stared at the barrier she'd erected, totally baffled. His entire impression of Jackie du Marcel was undergoing a radical change. They'd eaten together once or twice, and each time she'd seemed polished and poised and restless. She liked to laugh and tease and be the center of attention. Tonight, she acted totally different. Was that part of the reason he felt this odd pull of attraction, because she acted so differently? He'd thought her very much like his ex-wife and had kept a safe distance between them. Now he wasn't so sure. Jackie seemed softer, gentler. Yet just as flirty as ever if her eyes darting to his over the menu were any indication.

He studied the menu, trying to ignore the way she watched him. Had he been too long without a woman? Aware of every inch of the enchanting woman opposite him, he stirred restlessly in the hard chair. He raised his gaze, and clashed with hers.

When she smiled and looked down, fatigue fled. Suddenly he was wide awake, and definitely interested. He tossed the menu down on the table and leaned back, holding her gaze. What game was she playing now?

When Cade stared so boldly, Julianne dropped her gaze, feeling the heat and tension build between them. He thought she was flirting, she could tell. And if she had a clue how to proceed, she'd do it! But embarrassment burned in her cheeks. She only hoped that Cade attributed any heightened color to her being in the sun today.

The words on the menu danced before her eyes. She could not concentrate when he watched her so closely.

She couldn't believe she had dumped her purse! She was never that clumsy. And of all times to have a dozen packets of that flavored floss David gave her! She was lucky she didn't have one of his toothbrush bouquets along. Why hadn't she cleaned everything out before leaving home?

As the minutes ticked by she wondered how long she could hide behind the menu. Could she excuse herself, call a cab and reach home before Cade knew she'd left? Barring the door and never facing him again? So much for sophistication.

No, she had to brazen it out. Think! What would Jackie do? She almost groaned. First of all, on the short acquaintance with her sister before she'd left for Mexico, she definitely did not seem the type to be carrying floss with her, so a similar situation would never occur. And if it did, Jackie probably would have offered the floss to everyone sitting on the patio, laughing the entire time. Julianne should have tossed off the accident and acted as breezy as if that kind of thing happened all the time instead of running like a scared rabbit. She sighed softly, wondering if that was to always be her lot in life.

"Are you going to sleep over there?" Cade asked.

She lowered the menu a fraction. Smiling in what she hoped was an open imitation of her sister, she shook her head. Lowering her voice, she said breathlessly, "You'd know if I were getting ready for bed, Cade. I'm hungry, but not sure what I want."

Seeing Cade's eyes narrow she almost gave up. Obviously she might as well tell him who she was, he'd never believe she was her twin. How had Jackie maintained a casual friendship with the man? He was so handsome, even tired to death, Julianne just wanted to sit and feast her gaze on him.

"Have the burritos like you did last time and let's order. I'm fading fast."

"Does this work, staying awake so long so you can get back on California time?" she asked once the order had been placed. She'd been reluctant to release the menu. Its size afforded a safe place to hide and be hidden.

He grinned. "Hell if I know. I usually stop in New York and that helps the transition. But if I can make it a couple of more hours, I'll be able to get to bed and sleep until I wake up. I plan to unplug the phone, don't want the office waking me before I'm good and ready."

Feeling as awkward as if she were on a blind date, she sought a topic of interest. He'd asked about her family, could she ask about his?

"Tell me about your parents," she said, delaying her confession a bit longer.

He cocked his head, narrowing his eyes a bit. "My mother still lives in San Francisco."

"You say that like you've tried to get her to move here."

The waitress stopped and placed a huge basket of crisp tortilla chips and two containers of salsa, one red, the other green, in the center of the table. Julianne and Cade reached into the basket at the same moment, fingers tangling. Julianne snatched back her hand as if burned. Though the tingling that danced up her arm wasn't painful, it was disconcerting. Every nerve went on alert as she fought to keep her composure. What was it about this man that was so disturbing?

He looked at her oddly. Did he suspect?

"Mom says she prefers the old neighborhood. According to her, she's lived between the Martinellies and Burns for over twenty years, why should she move and start all over?"

"That's nice. That's part of the reason I didn't move far from home when—" Julianne stopped abruptly. She was so conscious of her body's reaction to Cade she could hardly concentrate. Jackie didn't live anywhere near their father's home. Fortunately Cade didn't find anything amiss from her statement. Distance must mean something different in California.

"I wanted to provide more for her than that old place. But she won't budge. I send her money, and she has some nice things in the house, and a man to come cut the grass in that postage-stamp yard. But she's content there. So I have to accept that. At least she isn't trying to grab everything she can and spend money like it's water,'' he finished.

''Who did that?'' Julianne asked, her interest captured once again. She enjoyed listening to Cade Marshall's strong, resonant voice. He could probably read a telephone book and she'd find it fascinating. She wondered if he'd ever tried acting.

''My ex-wife.''

''Oh.'' Caught by surprise, she didn't know what to say. Jackie probably knew all about his ex-wife. Unless he didn't talk about her often. Julianne wondered what the woman had been like, and why they'd divorced. If she ever married a man like Cade, she'd never let him go.

With sudden clarity, she stared at Cade Marshall and realized she could never marry David. She didn't feel about him as she should to be a proper wife. He would stay her friend, if he still wished to after she refused his proposal. But he was not the love of her life. She knew with certainty that until she found a man she loved passionately, she had to remain single. Smiling in sudden relief, she felt almost giddy. The trip to the West Coast had accomplished what she wanted. The question was settled. A huge weight lifted from her shoulders.

''Crystal was a liar and a cheat. I told you about her, when you asked about why I'm so adamant against lies—even polite social lies. She went into our marriage for the money and excitement. Prestige, if you like. But not for love of me. You must wonder about some of the men who date you, cupcake. You are beautiful and wealthy. Don't you wonder if you are being courted for yourself or for that money? Or to gain entry to Steven Bennet's world?''

It was a complaint her sister had voiced once.

She shrugged, his words echoing. *A liar and a cheat.* Julianne swallowed hard. She was both. She was lying by pretending to be Jackie, and was cheating him of the trust he held in her sister. Julianne shifted uneasily in her chair, glancing around at the crowd in the restaurant. Would Cade make a scene if she confessed her identity?

Better to wait, avoid it all together if she could. They were just having dinner. When he took her home, she'd make an excuse to avoid seeing him in the future and he need never know. She didn't want him to learn that she had lied. He'd be furious and she wanted to remember him as fun and intriguing, and for him to think well of her. Just this one night of playing a role, then she'd be herself again.

"Tell me more about working with special effects," she said brightly.

He smiled and leaned back in his chair, his eyes lazily tracking down her body. "How much can I explain with your lack of computer knowledge?"

Julianne started to interrupt. She knew quite a bit about computers—from setting up the new computerized catalog system in the library, to researching on the Internet. She clamped down on the urge to tell Cade about her expertise. She realized Jackie knew nothing about computers, so another near miss.

Cade explained how his programming skills resulted in the appearance of magical things, the different kinds of animation tools used to simulate actual people and events. Sometimes he stopped when Julianne wished he would delve further into the intricacies, but knew Jackie wouldn't have understood and was flattered he took the trouble to make sure his explanations were clear to someone he thought totally computer illiterate.

"Jackie! I thought it was you! Hi." A vibrant, red-haired woman dressed in black leather stopped by the booth, her smile wide and friendly. "I told Dolly it looked like you, didn't I?" She turned to the petite brunette beside her who nodded in agreement.

"Thought you were heading for Mexico for that film," she said.

Julianne's mind went blank. She stared at the women, noticing two men joining them, their faces friendly, open, smiling widely. Oh, God, these were friends of her sister's. Darting a quick look at Cade, she frantically scrambled in her mind for something to say. Was she to be exposed like this, in front of Cade and four of Jackie's friends?

"Hi, Cade. Do you remember us? We met at Jackie's party a few months back. I'm Sally McGuire. The handsome dude behind me is Toby Stanton."

Cade nodded and smiled easily. "I remember, and you're Dolly who works in advertising and your friend is Mark Harmond, in real estate, right, Mark?"

Julianne breathed a sigh of relief. She could not have bluffed her way through any introduction. Now what?

"The film?" Dolly asked again.

"Canceled," Cade said. "Just coming in?"

"Yeah, we're going to eat, then plan to go dancing. Want to join us?"

"I'll pass on the dancing, but you're welcome to join us if you like," Cade said, raising an eyebrow in question toward Julianne.

Julianne sat transfixed. Her heart raced as her palms grew damp. Rubbing them against her dress, she nodded and scooted over so Sally could slide into the booth beside her. Toby sat on the end while Dolly and Mark slid in to sit beside Cade. It was cozy, but not too crowded.

"We've ordered, so flag down the waitress and tell her to hold our order until yours is ready," Cade suggested.

"What's up?" Julianne asked quickly, hoping to get someone else talking before any questions were directed her way. She felt trapped. Somehow she had to bluff her way through this evening, or die of embarrassment.

"Nothing much. Dolly got that contract she's been angling for," Sally said, reaching for some of the chips.

"Great!" Julianne smiled at Dolly.

"Yeah, that's why we're here—celebrating. I'm treating. I'll treat you two, too."

"Quite a coup," Julianne said, hoping she was right.

"And a nice notice to the powers that be. I see great things for me now," Dolly said, beaming.

"You always did, kid," Mark added before he flagged down the waitress.

Toby asked Cade about his latest project, and they all listened while he spoke briefly about his Italian trip. Then the conversation veered to other topics. Julianne felt as if she danced through a mine field. She smiled, laughed and made as many comments as she could, none that had anything specific to say. She nodded, asked questions and soon fell into the sparkling mood of the evening.

She was having fun! These people were a bit irreverent about jobs and security, but they seemed to revel in having fun and experiencing life. They talked about vacations in Mexico, skiing in Tahoe, and a wide variety of topics concerning their different jobs. Julianne's staid life in Charlottesville seemed so quiet and dull after listening to the discussion swirling around her.

"Come dancing with us!" Sally said. Her sleek leather outfit covered her like a second skin. Julianne wondered what it would feel like to wear a leather skirt. Did Jackie have one in her closet? Probably.

"Thanks, another time," she demurred.

"Come on, Jackie, it'll be great. We'll bring you home afterward. Cade said he couldn't but that's no reason you can't come. Unless—" Suddenly Dolly looked uncertain. "Is there something going on between the two of you?" she asked.

Cade shook his head before Julianne could open her mouth. "No, just neighbors sharing dinner. We've come here once before." His eyes met Julianne's and she caught her breath at the look in them. "Right, neighbor?"

She nodded, mesmerized by the glint. Was he trying to say something with his look, or was she imagining things? She felt too uncertain, too keyed up to be sure about anything.

"I know you said you wanted to be an old lady before you

took the plunge again, but I thought…maybe…" Dolly trailed off, a rueful smile on her face.

Jackie looked at her and quickly picked up her cue. "I still do. Besides—" she looked at Cade in a decidedly flirtatious manner "—Cade's not interested."

"In you?" Sally asked, her eyes wide.

"In me or marriage," she replied.

All eyes focused on Cade.

"Thanks a lot, cupcake." He shrugged. "Once burned."

"Honey, don't let that stop you," Sally said, leaning across the table. "You look good enough to eat, and I bet the women would love to help you get over your divorce any way you'd like."

"Mostly by spending my money," he said easily. But there was a lingering touch of anger in the depth of his eyes.

"Prenupts. Solves everything." Sally waved her hand. "I did it the last time and when we broke up, no hard feelings."

"Sounds like you make a habit of marriage," Julianne murmured before she could stop herself.

Sally laughed. "Twice, as you know. Now I'm looking for the charm." She slid a seductive glance to Toby. "Right, Toby, love?"

"Don't look at me, Sally. Cade's got the right idea. Women want a man's money, and maybe something in the sack. Where's the loyalty and devotion that's supposed to go with marriage?"

The waitress interrupted, delivering the plates, warning everyone that they were hot. She refilled drinks, and the basket of chips, and left them to their dinners.

"I don't know why we're talking about marriage—none of us wants to get married anytime soon. I'm only twenty-six, I don't want to even think about it before I'm thirty," Dolly said, cutting into a huge burrito that covered most of her plate.

"What about a family?" Julianne asked. Having just made her decision about David, she had a lot of time to find a husband. But she wanted children and if she waited until she turned thirty, it would be that much longer before she had a baby.

Sally turned to look at her. "Thought you didn't want a kid."

Julianne shrugged. Had Jackie said that? They'd never discussed getting married or having children. Why would her sister resist a family? Julianne thought Jackie would want one more than most, having lived a rather disjointed existence with their father. Julianne knew she wanted a nice home and a loving family for herself, just like her mother and Gerald shared—complete with rambunctious boys and tomboy little girls.

"One day," Julianne hedged.

"Not me," Cade said.

"No children?"

He shook his head. "Too much can go wrong and the child ends up with just one parent. Or if there are financial problems, the kid suffers."

"With your setup, there'd never be financial problems," Julianne defended. Why should she care if Cade wanted children? They were just sharing dinner.

"Too risky. We can't predict the future, so how do we know?"

"Hey, I heard that Judee Falmouth landed that role on the soap she tried out for," Dolly said, changing the subject.

Julianne let the conversation swirl around, listening with interest to the gossip about mutual friends of her sister's. She felt a bit disoriented with the recent discussion. Didn't her sister want to marry, share her life with someone, and have a family? For an instant Julianne wondered if her upbringing in the picturesque town of Charlottesville influenced her desire for a traditional life.

Maybe it was a good thing she'd come to California. Having a chance to see how the other side lived might alter her own wishes for the future. And if nothing else, it clarified her thoughts for a marriage partner.

When they finished eating, Sally and Dolly urged Julianne to reconsider and come dancing, but she was firm in her refusal. They chatted as they walked to the parking lot, saying goodbye with promises to get together soon.

Slipping into the Porsche, Julianne welcomed the silence. The restaurant had been noisy, their conversation light and fast, and the quiet of the car seemed so peaceful. She leaned back and closed her eyes.

"Don't you fall asleep. If I start to doze, I need you to jerk me awake," Cade said as he slid behind the wheel.

"I'm not asleep, just relishing the silence. That place is noisy."

He looked at her. "I thought you like plenty of action, lights and activity."

Snapping her eyes open, Julianne stared at him. Damn, another near miss.

"I do. But this is nice, too," she said.

"You know, Jackie, you're a fraud," Cade said.

Julianne blinked, her stomach sinking. "What?" *He'd found out!*

"A fraud. You know—someone who pretends she's one way, but isn't."

"How did you guess?" she asked quietly.

He laughed. "It was a no-brainer. You flaunt yourself around like you're one hard babe, wanting parties and fast living. But look at you tonight, when it's one-on-one, you become almost tongue-tied. I suspect you are an old-fashioned girl at heart."

"Oh." Her heart pounded.

"Once your friends showed up, you were the old Jackie, laughing, talking, flirting. But when it's just you and me, you're almost like a different woman."

"Sorry."

"No, don't take it wrong. I liked it when it was you and me. But the change was something else." He frowned. "I can't remember that other time we went to dinner. Were you as quiet?''

"Of course not. I'm tired from being on the beach all day. Sunshine can wipe me out. I like having friends around. If you didn't want them to join us, you shouldn't have invited them to our table.''

"Come in for coffee when we reach home and we can talk for a little while. I'll try to stay awake,'' Cade invited as he approached their street.

"Just for a few minutes.'' She knew he was almost dead on his feet. The sooner he got to bed, the sooner she could escape. Her magical day was drawing to a close. Did Cinderella want the clock to slow down so she could savor every moment of the ball?

Cade's house was totally different from Jackie's. The old rambling Spanish style appeared more formal than Jackie's modern look. The heavy dark furniture looked solid and substantial, and carried with it the feel of permanence. He'd placed the sofa in front of a large picture window. She couldn't see out in the dark, but it faced the side away from Jackie's house. Did he have a garden, or was the view of the sea?

"Have a seat, I'll bring coffee in a minute.''

"Oh, Cade, don't drink any now, it'll keep you awake. I—''

"Maybe for two or three more minutes.''

Julianne frowned. "I shouldn't have come. You're so tired you look exhausted.''

Stepping to the door, she stopped when he leaned his hand against it.

Looking up, she found him close. Very close. Too close.

Taking a breath, she smelled aftershave and beer and the hint of masculine heat she'd felt on the beach. Fascinated, she watched as his green eyes studied every aspect of her face, as a painter might study a model. His left hand held the door closed, slowly his right hand came up and brushed against the edge of her jaw.

"Jackie," he said.

Swallowing, Julianne nodded. "What?" she whispered. Her hormones raced out of control again. Blood rushed through her veins, heat enveloped her and the desire to reach out and touch him almost overwhelmed her. She craved the feel of his lips against hers. He stood barely a foot away. If he leaned down just a bit and she stretched up just a bit—

He closed his eyes and half turned. "I'm so tired I can't see straight anymore. I'll walk you home."

"No, I'll just dash through the shrubbery." Julianne wrenched open the door and hurried down the walkway to the side of the yard.

He followed her and stopped at the edge of Jackie's yard, watching until Julianne had the back door open. She waved and dashed inside, closing it behind her and leaning on it. Breathing as fast as if she'd run the entire way, she willed her senses to return to normal. He was her sister's neighbor, for heaven's sake. They'd had dinner and now they were home. End of a perfect day.

But she wished he'd taken her into his arms and held her as if he'd never let her go.

For one moment she had thought he might do just that. Which would have been a major mistake. Until and unless she told him the truth about who she was, she couldn't continue to play games, to pretend to be her sister. He'd be furious, and rightly so. She hadn't meant to fool Jackie's friends, but it seemed easier than confessing in front of Cade and letting him discover her lie in a crowd of people. And she had wanted a day unlike anything she'd known. Sally had talked about her vacation in Cancún. Julianne had never met anyone before who so casually vacationed in Mexico.

Dolly's advertising job sounded glamorous and exciting. Not like hunting obscure facts for a university student's research project. They had invited her to join them dancing. The last time she and David had gone to the country club for a dance, she'd spent most of the evening listening to his discourse on a new methodology for tooth restorations.

If she'd gone tonight, would she have danced until her feet ached? She suspected it would have proved vastly different from the country club.

Pushing away from the door, Julianne checked the lock and headed for bed. She was tired, not fully used to California time herself. Tonight she'd get a good night's sleep and tomorrow avoid her next-door neighbor at all costs.

He didn't like liars and cheats. One strike against her. He was not interested in marriage. Not that she was either at this point. She hadn't even ended things with David—she couldn't be interested in any other man so quickly. And Cade didn't want children, which she did. So why were her thoughts a jumble?

Before getting ready for bed, Julianne opened her sister's closet and riffled through the racks of clothes. Discovering a leather skirt and vest, she took them into the bedroom. Taking off the dress she'd worn to dinner, she pulled on the skirt. It was snug, but moved easily when she walked. The vest covered her—barely. She suspected Jackie did not wear a blouse beneath it.

Studying herself in the mirror, Julianne couldn't help the flush of pleasure that stained her cheeks. She ruffled her hair, bit her lips to make them red, and then practiced a pouty, sultry smile. In front of her stood a woman men would want. Until she opened her mouth and had nothing to say. Then they'd instantly know the difference. Sighing, she turned away and began to unbutton her clothes. It was more than clothes, though. That loose and blousy dress tonight had given her a sense of adventure. And the confidence to bluff her way through the entire evening.

Was it only the clothes? Or was it a hidden desire to escape her quiet life in Virginia? Was she on a quest to find out who she was and what she wanted? It sounded like a lot for a vacation.

* * *

Cade stood beneath a hot shower, letting the water beat against his back. He braced his arms on the wall and shook his head to keep awake. Another five minutes and he'd be in bed and sound asleep. If he didn't wake for two days, it was fine with him.

He'd forget the problems with the Italian deal, forget the office for a while. And forget Jackie's weird behavior. And his attraction to her. When he awoke in the morning, everything would be back to normal and the Alice-in-Wonderland sensation of everything being topsy-turvy would have vanished along with his fatigue.

But he wished he'd kissed her one more time. She had stood by the door and looked up to him as if she would have said yes. The expression in her eyes had been unexpected. The few times he'd been around his neighbor, she'd laughed and flirted, taking nothing seriously. But today she'd seemed quiet, almost pensive. And he found it intriguing. What thoughts ran around in her head? Did she have dreams that beckoned, regrets over her marriage?

Did she, too, feel that pull of attraction that had surprised him? Her kisses on the beach had been hot and exciting, just what he'd expect from her. But was there anything more than mutual gratification?

Shutting off the water, he stepped out and quickly dried. Tossing the towel over a rack, he entered the bedroom. But he didn't head immediately for the bed. Instead, he veered to the window that looked out on Jackie du Marcel's house. A light burned in her bedroom. Was she going to bed now? Dressed in what? Not that terry robe. Did she sleep in the nude, or some frilly nothing of a nightgown? Or maybe a long, white cotton gown, sleeveless and loose, that found every curve and valley of her figure?

He groaned and turned for bed, this unexpected sexual attraction playing havoc on his senses. He wanted her. Nothing had changed from that morning. He should have pushed the issue. She was no shy miss. She'd been involved with several men. Tomorrow, if he felt the same, he'd push a bit more. If she was willing, then why the hell not?

Five

Julianne took a sip of coffee and gazed out the big kitchen window. The sky was a cloudless blue, the deeper tone of the Pacific sparkled beneath the sun. Another perfect day in paradise, she thought, drinking in the view as she savored her coffee.

Glancing at the clock, she saw it was almost nine. At noon, Virginia time, she planned to call David to refuse his proposal as gently as she could from three thousand miles away. Nervous, she sipped again. It would be awkward, and a bit sad. They'd been friends for so long. He took her to poetry readings at the university; she'd gone with him to parties the Masons put on. They'd shared meals, gone to the movies, played tennis at the local country club. Been a couple since she returned from college. It had been a nice, quiet relationship.

A bit predictable.

A bit dull.

She sighed. It wasn't his fault she yearned for more. Why wasn't she content with what she had? What if there were no knight in shining armor for her? What if David ended up being the only man to ask her to marry him?

Flicking another impatient glance at the clock, Julianne wished she could delay, but putting it off wouldn't change her feelings.

"Even if he is the only man to ever propose to me, I don't want marriage with David," she said aloud. "It wouldn't be fair to him or me."

The clock reached nine. She put down her cup and reached for the phone, dialing the familiar number.

"Dr. Hargrove's office."

"Is David around? This is Julianne Bennet," she said, gripping the receiver tightly.

There was a noticeable pause. Then, "Hold on, please."

Puzzled, Julianne wondered who answered the phone. It hadn't been Mattie Tomlinson, his receptionist. Julianne knew her voice.

"Hi, Julianne. How are you?" David's warm, friendly voice came across the line.

"David, I'm fine. I..." Now that the time arrived, she wasn't sure what to say.

"Having fun?" he asked. He had not understood her wish to visit her sister, especially before giving him an answer to his proposal.

"Yes. Yes, I am. David...I hope this isn't a bad time to call you."

"No, it's the lunch break. I don't have another patient until one-thirty. Stacey and I were just getting ready to eat."

"Stacey?" The hygienist? "Where's Mattie?"

"Gone for lunch, did you want to speak to her?"

"No, David. Actually, I called to talk to you." Julianne cleared her throat. "I've thought about your proposal. But I can't marry you," she blurted. Then closed her eyes in frustration. That was not the way she wanted to approach the subject. So much for finesse, for finding a kind way to reject his offer.

"Found someone else in California already?" he asked slowly.

Cade's image danced before her eyes. Rapidly Julianne shook her head. "No. No, there's no one else. I've been thinking about us. I don't think I'm ready for marriage, not yet." And not with you.

"We don't have to get married right away."

"No, David. It just wouldn't work." How could she explain without hurting him? "I'm sorry. I count you as one of my best friends. But I just don't see us married."

"Why don't we wait until you get home and discuss it?" he asked reasonably.

Hesitating, Julianne shook her head slowly, then realized he couldn't see her. "No. I don't want you to think I'm going to change my mind. You're a nice man, David. Find someone who will love you more than anything."

"I love you, Julianne."

"I love you, too, but as a friend. Not as a…a lover." She never pictured herself in bed with David. They'd shared a few kisses, nothing more. Yet since meeting Cade Marshall, she had no trouble imagining his kisses leading to much more— like touching her, caressing her, stripping her clothes from her body and following her down on a mattress where he'd make long, slow love to her for endless, wonderful hours.

She shivered. She shouldn't think about that, she was on the phone with David.

"I still think this is a bit sudden."

"I've been thinking about it since you proposed. And I'm sure. Thank you for asking me. I will hold it as a happy memory in my heart."

"Come see me when you get back," he said.

"Of course. I want to stay friends. Though I know we won't be as close as we've been. I understand that. But I cherish your friendship. Take care."

Julianne hung up the phone, feeling a mix of relief and guilt. He was a nice man. He deserved a woman who thought the sun shone out of him. Not a shy librarian who longed for more adventure and excitement in her life than he could provide.

Taking her cup to the sink to rinse it, Julianne looked over at Cade's house. There was no sign of activity. Had he left for work hours ago? Or was he still sleeping, trying to catch up? She wondered if he would think about her today. Though why should he? To him she was simply the same next door neighbor he'd known for a couple of years. A day spent together on the beach wasn't out of the ordinary enough to cause speculation.

Yet he'd kissed her. From what he'd said, he had never kissed Jackie. He seemed puzzled that there was any attraction. And reluctant to pursue it when she'd protested. Last night, she'd thought for sure he'd kiss her good-night when he stopped her from leaving his home. Though he'd come close to her, he hadn't kissed her.

Her heart raced at the memory of Cade standing so close.

Remembering the shimmering tingles that grew every time he came near, she wished she had initiated a kiss. She should have been more daring, followed up on his suggestion. Why couldn't she be more adventuresome? Innate shyness might have a place when living in Charlottesville, but she was on the West Coast now, pretending to be her much more experienced twin. Time she spread her wings and tried for that glamorous life she yearned for.

Right. What was the first step? She hadn't a clue. But one thing was for sure, she didn't plan to mope around her sister's house waiting for something to happen. She planned to stay in California just for the next couple of weeks. No time to waste mooning about a neighbor who'd had a free day on his hands and spent it with her.

Debating between shopping on Rodeo Drive or driving along the coast, she opted for driving the flashy convertible. It would be fun to explore the canyons of Malibu, then head south, bypassing L.A., to see more of California. If it rained one day, time enough then to go shopping.

The phone rang. She hesitated to answer it in case someone wanted Jackie. Yesterday had been exhilarating, pretending to be her sister. But she couldn't keep it up forever. On the other hand, it could be her mother, or even Jackie.

"Hello?"

"Jackie, my darling daughter, it's your father calling. How about lunch today at the studio lot? I have a small scene we're refilming because the stupid cameraman got the lighting wrong. You could meet me at one." The hearty, breezy voice was familiar. She'd heard it on the phone many times over the years, and had heard it loud and clear in movie theaters. Yet she hadn't talked to her father since last Christmas. He used to call on her birthday, when he remembered. But those calls had ceased when she'd turned nineteen. At least he couldn't forget Christmas.

"I could do that," she said cautiously. Would he want to have lunch with Julianne, or was he looking forward to seeing Jackie? Did he even know she had come to visit? Apparently not; he made no mention of including her in lunch plans. Would he be surprised to see her?

"One o'clock, then."

"Wait, where?" Jackie might know what studio, but Julianne hadn't a clue.

"At the studio cafeteria. You didn't spend all night partying, did you? I thought you gave that up after you and Jean split."

Julianne thought she heard a hint of reserve in his tone, but no censure.

"No. I was home quite early last night," she replied.

"Come to the gate on Sepulvada, I'll leave word that you're expected."

"See you at one."

She was going to have lunch with her father! Julianne leaned back and stared off into space. She'd missed her dad so much when her parents were first divorced. He'd always been so much fun. Mom had been left with most of the discipline. But over the years Julianne had grown used to his hectic schedule, his brief calls, his apparent lack of interest. Would today change that? Would he apologize for his neglect? Explain why he'd always been too busy to spend time with one of his little girls?

Not unless he knew who she was.

Of course he'd know instantly that she wasn't Jackie. She might have been able to fool a few of her sister's friends, but not their own father.

Julianne remembered once years ago when she and Jackie had been little. They'd tried to convince their father that they were each other—but he hadn't been fooled for a minute, despite his familiar assertion that they were as alike as two peas in a pod.

She might wear one of Jackie's outfits. And see how long it took him to uncover her disguise. A father would know his own daughter, even if he hadn't seen her in several years.

Looking forward to seeing him again, she wondered if he'd want to spend some time with her while she awaited Jackie's return. They could catch up on the last few years. Maybe she could even share a bit of her dilemma about Cade. He was a man. He could give her some advice.

Allowing herself enough time to find her way using the map she'd unearthed in Jackie's car, Julianne backed out the Mustang and headed toward Hollywood a couple of hours later. Wearing one of the silky jumpsuits Jackie seemed to favor, she smiled as the wind blew through her hair. This was the glamour she hoped for—dressing in designer clothes, driving a candy-apple-red convertible, lunching with a public figure. She felt as far from the shy librarian as she could get. For a moment she felt pretty and confident and carefree. It felt glorious.

Julianne found the gate with no trouble, and asked the guard directions to the cafeteria. Parking in one of the few empty parking slots, she hurried to the low building that catered lunch to the studio. Pausing inside, she looked around. She knew exactly what her father looked like from his last film. Spotting him seated near a window, she drew a deep breath and sauntered across the room. A wave here and there proved her sister was not unknown here.

"Hi," she said breathlessly as she slid into a chair opposite his, her eyes studying the man she hadn't seen in person since she was seven.

He glanced up from the menu he'd been skimming and smiled. "Hello. I wasn't sure if you'd left for Mexico yet or not. Heard Allie Adams got sick and I wondered if they would be shooting out of schedule, doing the other scenes first."

"Uh, yes, I heard that, too. I, um, I'll be leaving soon to do my bit."

He frowned and stared at her with a puzzled look, as if he found something wrong but couldn't identify exactly what.

Julianne took a breath and smiled. "So, what have you been up to?" How long before he recognized her? She leaned back, trying to appear calm and casual.

"Are you wearing different makeup?" he asked, studying her closely.

"Do you like it?" She tilted her head as if showing off. He suspected, but wasn't sure. She kept her expression as neutral as she could.

"You look a bit different. But I like it."

"Good. I'm glad you called for lunch."

It was enough to deflect his uncertainty. Steven Bennet launched into the reason he had to come to the studio, and why lunch was convenient. The movie currently being shot was chock-full of trials with some of the junior actors and problems with the weather and schedules. He complained, stopped to charm the waitress who took their order, then resumed once they were alone again.

At first Julianne listened avidly, then gradually grew conscious that her father seemed entirely self-centered. Throughout lunch, he dominated the conversation, taking it as his due that she would be fascinated by each word he had to say. Had he always been this way, even when married to her mother? Was this how Jackie had grown up? In vain, Julianne waited for him to ask her how things were going, to talk about any aspect of her life, to again look at her with a question in his eyes. Instead, Steven finished lunch with a quick kiss on her cheek and an admonition to keep in touch. He had to run for an appointment.

Julianne sat alone at the table after he left, stunned. She couldn't believe that he hadn't realized instantly that she wasn't Jackie. Yet upon some reflection, how could he? He had never asked after her, never showed any interest in what she was doing besides questioning why she wasn't in Mexico and if she wore new makeup. It seemed as if she'd served as a sounding board. Once he'd finished unloading, he'd left. He hadn't even made arrangements to see her again!

"Jackie?"

She turned and looked up, right into Cade's dancing green eyes.

"Hi." She smiled, glad she wore another of Jackie's creations. She chided herself. Did she really think he'd have any interest in a shy librarian from Virginia? Not when Hollywood overflowed with beautiful, talented and liberal women. Clothes didn't make that much of a difference, just in how she felt.

Cade pulled out the chair beside her and sat down.

"What are you doing here?" she asked.

"I met with a producer on a new script, then decided to stop by for a bite to eat. Saw you with your dad. He left, you didn't, so here I am."

"You could have joined us, eaten with us," she said, her pique with her father's behavior fleeing in the pleasure she found just being with Cade Marshall.

"Didn't want to interrupt."

"I don't think you would have," she murmured. "Just provided a bigger audience."

"What?"

Sighing gently, she shook her head in perplexity. "Honestly, he asked me to lunch, then spent the entire time complaining about his work, about how he's not getting the young hero parts like he used to, how he didn't like working with the director on the film. He never once asked about me or what I was doing."

"Sounds normal from what you said once before," Cade said easily. He flagged down a waitress and ordered a cup of coffee. The young woman refilled Julianne's cup when she brought Cade's.

Julianne wanted to talk to Jackie. Was this normal behavior for their father? She thought about her stepfather's interest in all his children, including her. The entire family gathered for dinner and everyone shared their day. Now that she'd moved out on her own, the ritual hadn't changed much. Anytime she visited, he was interested in what she'd been doing and her thoughts. He cared for her.

Maybe she had been the lucky one growing up. There was more to life than just having fancy cars and traveling to Europe. She wouldn't trade the love of her family for anything!

Looking up, Julianne saw Cade studying her.

"Do I have something on my face?" she asked, wondering why he stared so hard.

"No." Cade smiled and looked away. "What are your plans for the afternoon?"

"I plan to drive around. The weather is beautiful and I want to see as much as I can—" Oops, another faux pas. "I mean, with the top down and all. Did you catch up on rest from your trip?"

"I slept about ten hours, came into work late. Another couple of days and I'll be back on track."

"Maybe you should have taken a couple of days to get acclimatized."

"There's too much going on to goof off. And Pete's still having some minor glitches with the program in Italy. I want to be available if he needs resources from this end."

"Have you ever shown me your studio?" she asked, cocking her head to one side.

"What an odd way to ask. If you want to see the place, I'd gladly give you a tour someday. Thought you were more interested in live actors than cartoon characters."

"Is that a quote?" It sounded like something her sister might say.

"You made it."

Julianne shrugged her shoulders, remembering her vow to enjoy her vacation. Leaning forward, she gazed into his eyes. Her heart pounded so hard she could hardly think. Could he see how nervous she felt? "Then I would like to see it someday."

"You're on." Cade flung a few dollars on the table and took her elbow when she rose. "Maybe next Wednesday or Thursday?" he asked.

She felt his touch to her toes. "Sounds fine with me." She'd make sure nothing came up to interfere.

Weaving their way through the tables and the thinning lunch crowd, they moved to the exit and into the hot afternoon sunshine.

"Where did you park?" he asked.

"Over there." She waved her hand in the direction of the Mustang.

Rays of brassy sunlight bounced off the buildings; the air still and dry. Julianne hoped her sister had left some sunglasses in the car, it was almost too bright to see. When they reached the convertible, Cade hesitated a moment, slowly releasing her arm and turning her to face him.

"Busy Saturday night?" Cade asked.

"No." Truth to tell, she didn't ever have to be busy if Cade wanted to spend some time with her. Was he going to ask her out for a date? Anticipation bubbled up.

"I've been invited to a barbecue. I can bring a date, want to go?"

She smiled and nodded, surprised at the giddy excitement that she felt at the casual invitation.

"Phil Mott is throwing it. He and a couple of other guys share a big house in the San Fernando Valley. It'll take a while to get there, but should be a good party. Most of the office is going, and everyone is bringing at least one other person, from a different line of work. So there'll be plenty of variety."

"In other words, I don't have to worry about you all talking shop over my head," she said, delighted at the invitation. He must want to spend some time with her to invite her!

"Right. But there may be plenty of studio people, so don't you start talking shop," he teased.

His hard palms cupped her cheeks, his thumb brushing over the soft skin. "Cupcake, you make me wish I didn't have to go back to the office." His husky voice sent shivers of pleasure coursing through her. Knowing she wasn't the type to inspire silly names, she was touched more than she wanted to admit that he teasingly called her that.

Slowly he lowered his face to kiss her gently. His lips were warm and firm. He tilted her head slightly to better deepen the kiss, tracing her lips with the tip of his tongue, skimming the soft inner skin of her lower lip when she opened for him. With exquisite slowness, he explored her lips, her teeth, then plunged into the sweet heat.

The sun's brightness faded, a kaleidoscope of colors exploded behind her lids as she savored the sensations his kiss conveyed. She reached to embrace him, but he pulled back, gazing at her with a question in his eyes.

"Are you wearing some new perfume?" he asked, his hands releasing her, dropping to his sides.

"No, no perfume at all," she said. She didn't want the kiss to end, she wanted it to go on forever.

"I don't get it," he murmured.

"What?"

"Yesterday I thought it was because I was so tired."

"What was?"

"Wanting you."

Her heart skipped a beat, raced. Heat licked through her.

"Damn, I wish I could figure out just what game you're playing," he said.

"I'm not playing any game." Except being her sister. *Oh, oh, she should tell him!*

"I had one relationship with a beautiful woman and got burned. I won't do it again," he said sharply.

Beautiful? Her? "I'm not beautiful, it's the clothes," she said. No one had ever called her beautiful. David said she looked nice. Some of her dates in college had said she looked pretty. But beautiful?

He smiled sardonically, his eyes dancing in cynical amusement. "It's not the clothes, you are probably even more beautiful out of them. Shall I tell you a hundred times a day how beautiful you are?"

She blushed then looked away before she made a total idiot of herself. "I've got to go."

Cade stepped back and watched as Jackie drove away. She looked just like he'd seen her a dozen times before. Yet there was something different. Almost an air of innocence surrounding her. She'd seemed genuinely puzzled at her father's behavior. He was sure she'd mentioned Steven's propensity for egotism before. She'd laughed about it.

The biggest mystery, however, was his strong attraction. Why did she appeal to him in ways he couldn't even define? Some of the brashness and cocky sass he expected was missing. Poking fun at others didn't seem to be the norm these last two days. Nor being the center of attention. She had practically ignored the waves in the restaurant when she'd walked in. Was it all a ploy to capture his interest, or was there more to his sexy neighbor than he'd yet discovered?

Turning, he headed for his own car. He'd been hurt once by a fascinating woman, hadn't he learned anything? This was some trickery Jackie was up to, changing tactics, probably just to challenge his assertion he wasn't interested. Some women couldn't stand an indifferent man. Crystal had been that way. Once their marriage lost the early glow, she'd tried to reaffirm her own attractiveness by buying new clothes, constantly making a play for anything in pants, asserting her right to her own pleasure before all else—including their marriage vows. He wasn't going to fall for that again.

Dodging heavy traffic, Cade drove back to the building that housed his small company. He had plenty of time to think, and his thoughts kept returning to Jackie. Acting or not, she proved to be an intriguing woman. Maybe she was tired of the pretense. Maybe she was finally allowing the real woman to show through.

And getting involved didn't mean marriage.

He slammed on his brakes, narrowly missing the car ahead of him. Where the hell had that wild idea come from? Once lodged, he couldn't shake it. She knew the score. Hadn't one of her friends last night repeated her own vow to be an old lady before she ever considered marriage again?

And there would be no worry about the money. She was loaded if her life-style gave any indication.

He'd never noticed the same man hanging around, so she appeared fancy-free. Why not turn that fancy toward himself? If her intent was to gain his interest, she'd succeeded. He'd pursue her. A few kisses, some shared nights. Nothing permanent, nothing to catch the emotions, just enjoyment of each other's company.

Julianne stood on the edge of the deck feeling the afternoon breeze blow through her hair, gently toss the long skirt she wore. Her arms were a bit pink, as was her forehead, from her afternoon of driving, but she felt glorious. The soft cotton halter-neck dress caressed her skin as the wind blew it capriciously. She glanced down one more time. She did not have a halter bra with her and balked at wearing her sister's. Checking the mirror a half dozen times, she had almost convinced herself it wasn't noticeable. But she still had doubts.

What was it about living in California that made her so aware of sensations she'd never felt before? The wind caressed like a lover. The sun still bathed her skin with heat, and she felt every movement of the soft cotton. She stretched up her arms as if in worship, reveling in being a woman.

When she heard Cade's car door, she spun around, heart thumping. She knew she should tell him the truth but during her drive she'd decided to see him one more time. She *had* to. She had planned a nice stir-fry, had bought a light white wine. Of course he may have other plans, or just not want to spend an evening with her, but she had to try. She had rehearsed her invitation a dozen times. The worst that could happen would be he'd say no.

And there was still Saturday. Almost floating across the grass between their homes, she smiled when she first saw Cade. It seemed like longer than a day since they'd met. He held his sports jacket slung over one shoulder. Sometime on the ride home he'd loosened his tie so it hung lopsided from the open collar. He looked tired. He might want an early night, but he had to eat first.

"Hi," she called when he reached to unlock his front door.

He looked up, his eyes skimming across her from top to toe. A slow smile built. "Hi, yourself. What's up?"

Julianne stopped near the path, not trusting herself were she any closer. "I thought I'd invite you to share dinner with me, if you don't have other plans. To pay you back for last night."

"You don't owe me for dinner last night," he said slowly. The jacket slid off his shoulder and he caught it up in one hand. Leaning casually against the heavy wooden door, he crossed his arms and watched her as she approached.

"It won't be fancy, just stir-fry. Do you like that?" she asked, hoping she hadn't made a mistake in the food. If he didn't like Chinese she'd feel too awkward to change the menu just to get him to come to dinner.

"Love it. Give me a few minutes to shower and change and I'll be right over. Can I bring anything?"

"No. Just a healthy appetite."

She'd done it! Asked the most exciting man she'd ever seen to dinner and he accepted! Undoubtedly because he thought her the worldly Jackie, but that didn't matter. Her daring had paid off. Now if she could just think of something to talk about while they ate. She should have thought of that before. Now it was too late; her thoughts churned at the fact he was coming, she could not think up a coherent sentence.

Cade walked onto the deck a half hour later, dressed in pale faded denim pants and a loose pullover shirt with bold black and blue stripes. His hair appeared damp from his shower. She calmly greeted him. The serenity was a facade. Inside she roiled with conflicting emotions: delight he had come, fear she'd expose her deception—or worse, bore him to death. And shimmering over it all, a physical, sexual attraction that she couldn't deny no matter how hard she tried.

"I bought some wine, want some?" she offered. The glasses and bottle sat on the small wooden table between the chaise longues.

"Sure." He poured wine into both glasses and held one to her. When she took it, he touched the edge of his glass to hers. The soft clink sounded friendly in the afternoon sun.

"Cheers." He sipped appreciatively. "Mmm, good choice."

Julianne flushed with pleasure. There had been rows and rows of wines, mostly from California vineyards. She hadn't a clue what to buy until the owner had taken pity on her and suggested a couple of choices. Gratified that Cade approved, she sipped. The wine tasted delicious, fruity and a bit tart, but cooling on her lips and tongue.

She glanced at him, wondering what it tasted like on his tongue. God, she was acting like a schoolgirl. Her eyes met his. Curiosity shone from his, but he said nothing.

"I thought we could eat in a half hour. It'll just take me about fifteen minutes to prepare everything. The rice is steaming now. Have a seat." She sank gracefully into the lounge, tucking part of her skirt beneath her legs to keep it from flying up in the breeze.

"Pretty dress," Cade murmured as he moved the table and pulled his chair right up beside hers.

"Thanks." Glancing down surreptitiously, she double-checked the bodice. The cotton was thick enough and patterns swirled in blues and greens.

"You should wear dresses more often, they suit you," he said, with an appreciative look at her legs before moving his gaze out over the Pacific.

Julianne vowed then and there to wear only dresses for the remainder of her vacation.

"Tell me more about this barbecue we're going to on Saturday," she invited as silence stretched out comfortably between them. She felt a bit tongue-tied, on the edge of anticipation. She'd had David to dinner occasionally, but try as she might, she couldn't equate Cade with David.

"Phil Mott is throwing it. He lives with a couple of other guys in this huge house out in the Valley. They have a tennis court, swimming pool and big flagstone patio with a built-in barbecue grill that doesn't quit. Every few weeks they throw a bash. Usually, I don't go."

"Why not?"

He hesitated a moment, then said, "No date."

"I can't believe that!"

Rested, he looked devilishly handsome. His dark hair moved in the breeze, his eyes held mysteries she longed to uncover. Tall and lean, he appeared perfectly comfortable in a swimsuit on the beach or wearing the suit she'd seen him in today. Any woman would say yes in a New York minute to an invitation.

"Let's just say, no one I want to take—lest I give the wrong idea."

"I remember, you are not marriage-minded."

"No, I'm not. And a lot of women are these days. Hell, most are. So rather than start something I have no intentions of finishing, I just avoid the situation entirely. Once in a while, I go stag, but usually I avoid scenes like that.''

"Then I'm doubly honored to be invited," she said.

"So you should be. But I think I'm safe. In the two years we've been neighbors, you've never come on to me. And after last night, I can guess why. You're not an old lady yet—so too early to marry.''

She smiled and nodded. Jackie was probably having too much fun to settle down, and Julianne planned to have the same kind of fun. Maybe when she was thirty or older she'd want to settle down, but for now, she was free and could be as wild as she wanted. Or as she dared.

Six

Cade touched her shoulder. "You're sunburned."

Julianne jumped. "Yes. I drove around this afternoon with the top down never thinking how burned I'd get. If I do it again, I'm either wearing long sleeves or will slather on the sunscreen."

"Where did you go?"

"Oh, just around."

"No tennis match?"

"What?"

"Didn't you tell me a few months ago that you were spending a lot of time at the tennis club down on Mulholland?"

"Did I?" She looked away from his penetrating gaze. "Not today. I haven't been in a while." But she enjoyed tennis and was pleased to learn Jackie did, too. Maybe she could use Jackie's membership and play a few sets some afternoons. Time hung a bit heavy with her sister gone. The kitchen timer chimed.

"Oops, time to get busy." Julianne escaped into the

kitchen, placing her almost-empty wineglass on the counter. She had set the dining room table for the meal, feeling it was too windy on the deck.

Running her fingers through her hair, she wondered what it looked like. Did she have time to dash upstairs and run a brush through it?

"Can I help?" Cade followed her in, his glass and the wine bottle in one hand.

"No, you're the guest. I can manage."

"I'm sure you can." Something in his tone caused Julianne to spin around and look at him.

"What?"

"I'll admit being surprised you're so efficient and organized. I've always pictured you a bit helter-skelter—doing things at the spur of the moment, at the last minute."

"Inviting you was a spur-of-the-moment thing."

He nodded. Placing the wine and glass on the breakfast table, he spun a chair around, straddled it and rested his stacked hands on the high back.

"Have you made stir-fry before?" he asked lazily.

"Sure, a million times." Julianne was comfortable in the kitchen. She turned back to the stove, glad to have something to do besides stare at her sister's neighbor. Smiling in simple joy as she prepared the meal, she almost pinched herself to assure herself the evening was real. She was in California, preparing dinner for a man she'd only met yesterday. It was just as she'd always pictured her sister.

Cade proved attentive and easygoing during dinner. If he looked at her oddly from time to time, Julianne ignored it. The magic in the air thrilled her. Conversation proved easy as they moved from books they enjoyed to a discussion of how different books could be made into feature films. Julianne forgot she was a rather shy librarian from Charlottesville, Virginia. She talked easily, flirted a bit and covered her own shyness with the mantle of worldly Jackie du Marcel.

"Want to take a walk?" Cade asked as they finished their coffee.

"I would love to." The two glasses of wine made her feel warm and mellow. Cade's presence notched up the temperature. She quickly stacked the dishes in the sink as the thought of a moonlit walk along the beach hummed through her.

"Do you think I need something for my arms?" she asked when ready.

"No. The wind's died down, and it's still warm out."

He took her hand casually as she passed through the door, lacing his fingers through hers. Slowly they walked to the cliff and down the rock stairs. The soft crash of surf provided a gentle background to the waning twilight. The sunset had been spectacular, the sky still showed a hint of lingering color. High over the bluff the full moon shone, its light growing brighter as the sky darkened.

Julianne kicked off her sandals when she reached the bottom, noting Cade had slipped off his shoes. The sand held the day's warmth as they walked toward the water. It grew damp and firm close to the water's edge. Cade headed south. The surging and retreating surf sprayed mists that hovered, cool in the gentle stirring of the evening air.

"I love the beach," Julianne said, breathing deeply. "If I could, I'd live—" Stopping instantly when she realized where her thoughts were leading, she glanced up at Cade. Had he noticed?

"Live here and never travel?" Cade asked.

"Right."

"I thought you enjoyed staying in France several months a year. You said last summer that there was no city like Paris," Cade said. He kept an eye on the waves, making sure to keep away from the grasping reaches of the spent breakers.

"That's certainly true," Julianne hedged. Her best bet was to keep her mouth shut. And that wouldn't be hard. Joy built as they walked silently along the deserted beach. The sky was crowded with faint stars, overwhelmed with the bright shining moon. It lacked only a day or two to fullness, its light coating everything with a silvery radiance.

"I feel like it's magic," she said softly. "Maybe I'm Cinderella."

Cade spun her around in front of him. "Cinderella needs a ball. May I have the honor of this dance, my lady?" He bowed slightly, then released her hand to take her into his arms. "Know any good slow tunes?" he asked whimsically, swaying without moving his feet.

Julianne laughed softly, extremely conscious of his warm hand against the bare skin revealed by the low back of her dress. Her breasts pressed lightly against his chest, tingling and filling. She yearned for a closer contact, but couldn't possibly initiate one. "No songs, what do you suggest?"

Humming a familiar waltz, Cade moved in time to the melody, dancing in and out of the spent waves, on the hard-packed sand. Up and down the beach, around and around they danced. Julianne let her head fall back as she gazed at the velvet sky speckled with glittering stars. Cade's voice and the sound of the sea mingled to provide a melody she'd never forget. It was magic and she became enchanted. Dancing in the strong arms of the most handsome man she'd ever seen, the two of them in a world of their own at the edge of the earth—nothing beyond but sky and sea and endless eternity. This was bliss.

Savoring every second, she knew she'd never felt so free or joyful, never so light and graceful. This was what she missed with David. This was the intangible something she felt as if she had been missing all her life. Glorious! She had never enjoyed herself so much, or felt so alive. Every nerve ending tingled with sensuous awareness for the man who held her. When her legs brushed his, she shivered. His hand never let her stray more than a few inches. Her own inclination kept her close.

"Happy?" Cade asked softly, indulgently, when the song came to an end.

"Yes! I've never danced in the moonlight by the edge of

the sea. Maybe I'll include it in my things to do from now
on!'' Almost giddy with delight, Julianne twirled around, and
danced a few steps on her own. She wanted to embrace everything, hold it all close to her heart for all time. Stopping,
she grinned at Cade. ''Do you think I'm totally nuts?''

He shook his head. ''What I think is that I have known you
for two years and never had a clue about you. Which is the
real Jackie du Marcel? Rich and sassy jet-setter, or a woman
who likes simple pleasures like a walk on the beach?''

''Can't I be both?'' she asked, keeping her distance as the
magic faded and reality returned. She didn't want him to look
too closely. Would he discover the fraud? She was not her
sister, and it obviously showed. But she didn't care. Not for
tonight. A spell captured her, held her in thrall as she reveled
in the mystery of the evening. Time enough for reality when
they returned to the real world. This fantasy would only last
a bit longer. Maybe by midnight, the spell would end and
she'd be herself again.

''A person is not just one thing. Not just a jet-setter or a
dutiful daughter. She can offer a different facet on different
days, do things in the moonlight with abandon that might not
be possible by daylight. Don't you think?'' she asked.

''Like being an enchanted princess dancing on the edge of
the world?''

''Exactly—that's what I feel like right now! Isn't it wonderful?'' Julianne laughed from sheer joy and spun around like
a ballerina. Her arms out, her head flung back to the sky, she
spun around and around, faster and faster, feeling almost as if
she could fly!

Until she tripped over a sharp shell and fell flat on her back.

The frothy, foaming water reached up the beach with gleeful
success and soaked her from head to toe.

''Oh, no!'' Julianne scrambled up before Cade could reach
her, but the damage had been done.

''Are you all right?'' Reaching out, he grabbed her arms,
studying her in the moonlight.

"Sure, if you like drowned cats. I stepped on a shell or something." She lifted her foot to see if she'd cut it. Cade knelt in the wet sand and took her foot in his warm hand. Running his thumb across the bottom, he looked up. Water wet his trousers, swirled around her ankles.

"No cuts. Can you walk?"

"Of course." She put weight on it. A small twinge the only residue. Smiling shakily, she stepped back, water dripping from her hair onto her shoulders. The evening air that had seemed so warm, now chilled. She shivered with cold.

"Come on, you need to get inside and into something warm." Cade took her hand again and they started back.

Walking briskly for speed and warmth, Julianne couldn't help berating herself for her clumsiness. Her perfect evening was ruined. She'd been having such a wonderful time. She would be willing to bet lunch that her sister had never fallen in the water when out with a man she was trying to impress.

Trying to impress? Well, of course, she was. Dynamic and entertaining as Cade was, of course she was fascinated with him. Thrilled he had spent the evening with her. Embarrassed, heat rose to her cheeks, providing warmth of the wrong kind. She wanted to run to the house and hide. Try to forget her lack of sophistication. Nothing to do but brazen it out at least until she reached the house.

Cade snatched up their shoes when they reached the stone steps. "Can you manage in bare feet?" he asked.

"Sure, the steps are smooth and the grass is soft," she said, stepping on the first one. Truth to tell, she didn't want the delay of putting on shoes. She just wanted to get inside, close the door behind her and block this from her memory.

When they reached the patio, light spilled from the windows, illuminating the flagstone with a soft radiance. Julianne stopped just out of the light's beams, and turned to Cade. "I can manage from here. Sorry to end the evening so soon. I'm glad you came for dinner."

He offered her her sandals, and Julianne hooked them over her finger.

Tilting her head, he looked into her eyes. "I had a wonderful evening. Your dinner was delicious, but I enjoyed the company more."

Until your hostess fell in the water, Julianne wanted to scream. It wasn't fair—she had just wanted one perfect evening.

Cade leaned closer and kissed her. His lips were warm against her cool mouth, and moved with coaxing intensity. Slowly, so slowly she didn't even realize at first what he was doing, he pulled her into his arms, wet hair, soaking dress and all. His tongue traced the outline of her lips, until she gave in to the persuasion and opened her mouth slightly. There was no quick move. Slowly Cade touched the soft inner lip, rubbed against her teeth, then slipped in to deepen the kiss.

His hands pressed her against him as his fingertips massaged her cool skin, rubbing from shoulder to bottom. Heat trailed his touch, and desire blossomed. When one arm moved around her ribs, skimming over her wet dress, Julianne gave way to the growing craving and reached up to encircle his neck, sandals dropping unheeded onto the flagstone. She pressed a bit closer, reveling in the myriad sensations that clamored for attention. Warmth filled her chilled body, excitement replaced embarrassment, desire flared and staggered her. His hands felt hot against the damp fabric, matching the flame building inside.

Cade trailed kisses on her cheeks, her jaw, the pulse point at her throat, slowly making his way up her neck to find her lips again. His hands caressed until he pulled back a bit and cupped one breast. His thumb brushed lazily over the turgid peak. Julianne shivered and broke away, stunned at the reaction of her body. She hardly knew the man, had never thrown caution to the wind in this manner. Though for a few moments she almost demanded he come inside with her and stay the night. A few heated kisses couldn't have her changing the precepts of a lifetime.

"I can't do this," she whispered, then turned and ran into the house. Without pausing, she went up the stairs and into her sister's room. Closing the door, she hurried to the bathroom and shut that door, leaning against it as if holding it against a predator. There was no sound save her own harsh breathing. Slowly she flicked on the light.

She was an idiot. A total and complete ninny! He'd merely kissed her and she had bolted like a scared rabbit. Mortified, she wanted to turn back the clock and start over. She'd make sure they never left the patio. A mere kiss should not wreak such havoc.

Well, maybe a *mere* kiss was a bit of an understatement— that kiss had been unlike any she'd ever experienced. But she couldn't just fall into bed with a man who kissed like that.

She closed her eyes in embarrassment. Maybe he hadn't even wanted to go to bed. Maybe he had been caught up in the kiss as she'd been and his hands had roved. Wow, had they roved! Touching her in ways no one else ever had. And provoking shimmering feelings that she'd never known existed. Even now after fleeing like a rabbit, her body hummed.

"And now I've acted like the naive girl I am and he'll probably never want to see me again. Oh, God, we're supposed to go to that barbecue on Saturday. I'll have to cancel. Or maybe he'll cancel." The thought didn't bring the relief she hoped for. "How can I just treat this like nothing happened? I can't face him again. I can't!"

Shivering in her wet dress, she caught sight of herself in the mirror and was horrified. The dress might as well have been a second skin, leaving nothing to the imagination. Her nipples pushed against the damp cloth, cold and tight and throbbing. Her skirt clung to her legs, outlining each one, molding them. Even the outline of her panties showed through.

Ripping off the offending dress, she wadded it into a ball and tossed it across the room. Running the shower, Julianne stepped in, turning the water hotter and hotter until the chill began to fade. After a few minutes she almost laughed aloud. She had mentioned Cinderella on the beach, but she was Cinderella in reverse. Starting out looking nice, she ended up looking like a bag lady. So much for romance and fantasy. Maybe that kind of thing only happened in books. Real life had a way of interfering with romance.

Sighing, she turned off the water and got out. She towel-dried her hair, combing it back from her face. Dressing in her sleep shirt, she slowly wandered downstairs. Might as well do the dishes and tidy the kitchen. She hated coming into a mess in the morning.

Cade sat at the breakfast table, his long legs stretched out before him. His feet were bare, a light dusting of sand coated the tops. Looking up when she entered, his expression seemed thoughtful.

"Oh." Julianne stopped short. She thought he'd gone home.

"You all right?"

She nodded, then glanced down at the sleep shirt. "Go home, Cade," she said. Hair still damp and slicked back, a faded T-shirt from the university, bare feet and no makeup. No woman wants a man to see her like that, not when she's interested in making a good impression, not scaring him to death.

"You look cute," he said, rising.

"Cute is not the image I'm looking for," she said petulantly.

He laughed and walked over. His forefinger tilted her chin until she faced him. "Well, it will have to do for tonight. Warm enough, now?" he asked.

She nodded. If she opened her mouth, she'd probably start wailing at the turn of events. Did this just point out how unsuitable she was for life in the fast lane? Or was it a question of practice? Would she be in California long enough to find out?

His thumb brushed against her lips. The heat that coursed through her had nothing to do with her recent shower.

"You fascinate me," he said slowly.

"You're pretty fascinating yourself," she said.

"My life is an open book."

"Turned to one page only. What do the other pages hold?"

"Want to find out?"

She nodded, afraid yet unable to help herself. She wanted to learn everything there was to know about this man. Explore the sensations that he evoked, discover what caused this attraction, and decide what to do about it. Time was limited, experience was almost nil.

"I'll pick you up around four on Saturday. We'll drive to Phil's party and just enjoy ourselves, what do you say?"

Julianne nodded. This encounter was going better than she'd anticipated. And she'd not been embarrassed, after all, something about Cade made her feel different. Things had to get easier. And she had to decide what she was going to do. She knew Jackie would never bolt from a kiss. She probably would institute another one right now and go as far as Cade pushed.

"Good night." He gently brushed his lips against hers and turned.

Julianne watched him walk away and she sank into a chair. Her knees seemed as weak as wet spaghetti, her heart raced, and her lips tingled. Saturday seemed a long time away.

Cade stepped out onto the patio and walked away from the light. Pausing at the edge, he circled back and stepped close enough to peer in through the window. Jackie sat in a chair, staring out at the night. He watched for several minutes, but when she made no move, he turned to head for home. She hadn't shifted an inch the entire time. He'd give a lot to learn what thoughts tumbled around in her mind. Gloating over getting him interested? Or was there something else going through that pretty head of hers?

He tried to remember everything he'd been told about his

neighbor. They had met casually when she'd first moved in, only two months after he had bought his house. Because she traveled a lot, she asked if he would keep an eye on her place, even giving him a key. He'd done a bit more traveling in those days, and had reciprocated. Beyond that, the entire first year he doubted if they had exchanged more than a few words.

After her return from France last summer, she had invited him a couple of times to parties. Her friends were young and ambitious. Few were connected with the film world, which had surprised him given she played bit parts and given the success of her father. But the people he'd met at her house came from all different professions. He'd had the best conversation with a landscape architect at one party. They really clicked. He should have followed up and called Joel again.

Maybe he would, and casually bring the conversation around to Jackie.

He hadn't cared to find out the details about his neighbor before. But then, he hadn't felt this strong pull of attraction, this sense of...of almost recognition. As if he had known her before. Feeling comfortable around her, feeling connected somehow.

Which showed he was still suffering from the rigors of jet lag.

Jackie represented the epitome of the type woman he'd sworn to avoid. Crystal had been the same. Always out for gaiety and excitement. The more money spent, the better. The faster the car, the higher the thrills, the more Crystal craved excesses. Superlatives. And Jackie had always struck him as having a similar viewpoint of life.

Yet a lot of things didn't add up.

And he would swear the expression in her eyes when she'd bolted from the deck had been sheer panic. Was she leading people on? Creating some sophisticated facade to hold the wolves at bay? Feigning a level of experience to cover a lack? To hide the innocence that peeked through now and then?

Innocence? Jackie had been married to that Frenchman.

Cade had a hard time convincing himself that she had any innocence left.

He let himself into his house. Stopping only long enough to pour himself a snifter of brandy, he headed for his bedroom. He needed a few more nights of rest before he was operating on all cylinders again. Sipping the brandy, he shed his clothes, his eyes going from time to time to the light shining from her bedroom.

Innocence peeked out now and then. He recognized it, just not the reason. Was it all a game? He had to admit she confused the hell out of him. Every time he expected her to act one way, she acted differently. Instead of pegging her for another Crystal, she gave off conflicting signals. One moment, brash sassiness. Another, a sweetness that was almost a lost trait with the women he knew.

The hell of it was, he almost didn't care if she were playing a game. He wanted her.

And he planned to have her.

When the ride was over, if he got burned, he'd make sure it was worth it.

He stood by the window, sipping the last of the brandy. One by one the lights downstairs flicked out. He could imagine her progression to her bedroom. Would she go right to sleep, or read for a while? Did she have a television in the room, a stereo? He wondered about her habits, the patterns and routines in her life. Did they vary when she visited France? Was she methodical about some things or spontaneous in everything?

The bedroom light went out.

Slowly Cade turned and headed for his bed. Flipping on the light by the phone, he looked up her number and dialed.

It rang for a long time. Had she fallen asleep so quickly?

"Hello?"

"Hey, cupcake, it's Cade."

"Oh, did you forget something?"

"No, just wanted to call."

"I'm in bed."

"I know. I can see your bedroom from mine. I saw the light go off."

"You can see my bedroom?"

He almost laughed. For a moment he envisioned her sitting up in outrage and indignation. Probably that flash he was growing familiar with sparked in her eyes.

"Just a bit from my bedroom."

There was a background rustle. "I see your light is still on," she said.

He leaned back against the headboard and flicked the light out. "Now we are alone in the dark."

"Can you actually see into my bedroom?" she asked.

"Why, are you wearing nothing?"

"No, I'm wearing my nightshirt."

He chuckled at the primness in her tone. "It's a very nice shirt, fits you so well."

"It's big and loose—"

"And soft cotton that clings to your body like a lover."

"Oh."

He smiled again, suddenly wishing he'd stayed longer. He would like to see the confusion in her eyes, the soft shyness that sometimes flared up. The innocence. "Aren't you going to ask me what I'm wearing?" he teased.

"Probably nothing," she murmured.

"Right first time."

"Oh-hh." There was background noise again.

"Where are you?" he asked, dropping his voice into a softer tone.

"I just got back into bed and covered up. You should do the same."

He laughed. "God, you sound as prissy as a maiden aunt. I am in bed. But not covered."

"I can't talk anymore," she said hastily.

"Why not?"

"I—" The silence stretched on forever. Then he heard a soft click.

He laughed and tossed the phone on the bedside table. How much had been put on and how much genuine? It didn't matter. She knew how to push his hot buttons. Would she open the door if he stormed over right now? Or would she play coy a bit longer? He could wait. Barely. Saturday was only two days away. Anticipation would make their coming together all the sweeter.

Julianne avoided the window the next morning while she dressed, then went to look over at Cade's house. It looked still. No lights shone, but the bright sun would make lights unnecessary. He'd gone to work.

After a light breakfast, she pulled Jackie's address book over and looked through it to see if she could find the name of the tennis club. Maybe she could go and find someone to play with. No doubt Jackie had some regular friends, but Julianne didn't begin to know who to call. If she could just drop by the club, chances were that she'd find a pickup game.

She reached for the phone when it rang.

"Hi, honey." Her mother's cheerful voice came across.

"Mom, is something wrong?"

"No. Can't a mother call to say hi? I'm missing you, darling."

Julianne usually spoke to her mother almost every day, if only for a few minutes. It was more habit than a real need, but maybe that was only on her part. Her mother might feel differently.

"I'm glad you called. I broke it off with David," Julianne said. "You and Gerald should probably know in case you run into him."

"Oh, honey, David's so nice and steady."

Julianne grimaced. "Too much. I want a bit of excitement in life."

The silence on the other end was telling.

"Not as much as Jackie. But more than what I have," she said to fill the dead air.

"It's natural, I guess. For the young."

"Mom, how did you and Dad meet? You two come from such different backgrounds, I'm only now realizing how far apart you were."

"I visited my aunt Marilyn in New York. Your father was an actor just starting out in some off-Broadway production. We met, fell madly in love and that was that."

"Did you enjoy the excitement?" Julianne asked slowly.

"At first. It was so different from Lynchburg. But once you girls were born, I wanted more of what I knew as a child, stability, roots, family ties. Your father never wanted that. He was, and still is I suppose, quite content to play all the time. Excitement was like an elixir for him."

"So after the divorce you went home to Lynchburg."

"We went to Lynchburg. A few months later I met Gerald and fell in love all over again." Her voice softened. Julianne never doubted the love between her mother and her stepfather, it was evident whenever they were together, or spoke of each other.

"But Charlottesville is a bit—" She couldn't call it dull. It had been her home for years.

"A bit quiet if you are comparing it with L.A. Yes. And maybe you need to fly a bit before settling down."

"I'm having a wonderful time. Yesterday I drove Jackie's car. The boys would die to have a ride in it—a candy-apple-red convertible."

"Don't tell them or they'll bug us to death to visit Jackie. Have her come here, she could drive the car."

Julianne laughed. "I think she moves a bit faster than driving a car from California to Virginia. But I'll tell her."

"And the neighbor? Have you seen more of him?"

"Actually he invited me to a barbecue some friends of his are giving on Saturday. It's in the San Fernando Valley." For some reason she didn't want to discuss dinner last night. Not yet. Some memories were so precious, and the rest were too embarrassing.

"I remember the Valley. Maybe you'll meet other people you can do things with. When is Jackie returning?"

"I don't know. Whenever her scenes are in the can, I guess."

Peggy laughed. "How like your father you sound. Have you seen him?"

"Yes. We had lunch yesterday. He, um, he talks about himself a lot."

"You should have been a diplomat, darling. He sounds as if he is as self-absorbed as ever. Don't be too disappointed."

"I'm not for me. But I realized Jackie must have missed what I had growing up. You and Gerald were always interested in what I was doing. Still are. I don't think Dad particularly cares what she does."

Peggy sighed. "That was the primary reason I thought she rushed into that marriage with Jean—her search for someone to care for her."

"Mmm."

"Got to run, honey. I'll call in a few days, just wanted to make sure you were okay."

"Thanks, Mom. Tell everyone there I send my love."

Julianne hung up, thinking about her mother and father. They had been so different. As different as she and Cade? He lived in a world she only dreamed about. And she lived in a world he had never known. Growing up in sophisticated San Francisco, working and living in jaded Los Angeles, how would he relate to the quiet, slow pace of life in a sleepy Virginia college town? Or to someone who grew up in that town?

Seven

Julianne found the address of Jackie's tennis club. Locating her sister's racket, she changed and headed out. Luck was with her. When she arrived at the club, she was greeted by name—her sister's name, that is—as soon as she walked in. When asked if anyone was looking for someone to play, she was immediately paired with a new member, Becky Foster. Relieved she didn't have to pretend to be other than herself, she enjoyed the sets. Becky was a better player than Julianne, but had not won every game. They stopped when the heat became too oppressive and shared lunch.

Heading back for the house a couple of hours later, Julianne considered her day. Not very different from a weekend in Virginia. Her parents belonged to the country club, she had a membership, as well. Even as a young teenager she'd spent many Saturdays at the club, either in the pool or on the tennis courts. She'd tried golf a couple of times, but didn't enjoy it as much as other activities.

Some things didn't change with different states and backgrounds. She'd enjoyed the exercise, and getting to know Becky. It had been awkward when they'd parted. Julianne said she'd try to call, but wasn't sure how long she would stay. Lunch had emphasized how lonely she was. She'd come to visit her sister, and instead rambled around alone in the big house.

Of course with Cade next door, she could always dash over to visit. But she wouldn't. She was getting too involved with her sister's next door neighbor. There were other things to do besides having him entertain her.

She knew where he wanted to entertain her, and once in a while she almost forgot why that wouldn't be such a good idea.

Like now. She was on vacation, beholden to no one. Telling David she could not marry him had cleared that obstacle. Young, with few obligations, she was as free as she would ever be in her life. Why not enjoy whatever Cade had in mind?

Because you'd make a fool of yourself, that's why, she softly chided. Last night had been a prime example. She'd fled like a scared rabbit just because he wanted to take the kiss a bit beyond her experience. She'd been scared silly. How could she pretend to be some kind of femme fatale if she bolted every time she got in over her head?

What would Jackie do?

She didn't know her sister as well as she would have had they grown up together like most twins. They had talked on the phone at length. Yet that alone wasn't enough. Julianne had a pretty clear understanding of her sister—even as small children, Jackie had been the adventuresome one, Julianne more timid.

The answering machine blinked steadily when Julianne entered the house. She punched the rewind button and listened to the messages. The first was from someone named Bart, calling Jackie about a reference. Next Sally's voice, insisting Jackie join them tonight, they were going party hopping and she had to come. Toby would come for Jackie after he picked

her up and she'd have nothing to do but be ready by seven.
The third message sounded like a sales pitch and Julianne shut
the machine off.

She wandered upstairs, the tantalizing thought of party hopping filling her mind. She had pulled off the impersonation at
dinner, not a single one of Jackie's friends had suspected.
Could she do it again tonight? Jackie apparently had a huge
circle of friends. The parties would be lavish and undoubtedly
a lot of fun. She'd just be one of the crowd, mingling with
people she hadn't known all her life, seeing how Californians
lived. Why not go? If Jackie had been home, Julianne was
sure she would have gone and taken her twin with her.

Why not go as Jackie? She wasn't hurting anyone. Julianne
decided she'd do it. She'd be ready when Toby arrived and
gain a bit more insight to her sister's life-style.

It took much longer than Julianne would have expected to
find the right thing to wear. She wanted something different
from her normal attire, something of Jackie's that would reflect
the personality she often wished she possessed. Trying on
dresses, pants, skirts and tops, she finally selected a flirty red
skirt that barely covered her decently. Matched with a lacy
black crochet top, she felt daring and provocative. After her
shower, she carefully applied her makeup. Frowning in dissatisfaction, she scrubbed her face. Rummaging around in her
sister's cabinet, she tried a bit of this and that. The result was
more than satisfactory.

Dramatically highlighting her eyes, she looked mysterious
and worldly. The lipstick matched the skirt, hot red, and the
effect on her lips startled her. Pouting provocatively, she swept
her lashes up and grinned. One hot babe here! Brushing her
hair until it swirled around her in a tousled mane, she was
more than satisfied. She looked just like her sister, nothing
like a quiet woman from a small Southern town.

The high-heeled sandals completed her quest. She posed in
front of the mirror, turning this way and that, struck by every
angle. Forget safety and conservatism. This was one reason

she'd come to California. This woman was ready for life in the fast lane.

When the doorbell rang a few minutes later she hurried down the stairs, conscious of the flutter of her short skirt, of the long expanse of tanned legs. She slowed when she reached the entry hall, no sense arriving out of breath. Toby was the name of the man coming to pick her up. And Sally would be with him. Others? She'd have to listen carefully to pick up names and garner some sort of clue about whom the people were and what they did. But it added to the fun. She was on an adventure the likes of which she'd never imagined a few days ago.

"Going somewhere?" Cade leaned against the doorjamb when she opened the door.

"Oh." She had not expected to see him before tomorrow. "Hi. Yes, actually, I'm going to a party. Come in."

"I won't keep you. Thought you might like to grab a hamburger or something, but you've got plans."

"It's a last minute kind of thing," she said. The bright anticipation of the evening dimmed a bit. She'd like to have dinner with Cade rather than party with a bunch of strangers. Biting her lip in indecision, she wondered if she could cancel the party hopping.

"You look great," he said, his gaze moving leisurely down her body.

Julianne resisted the temptation to stand taller, to make sure he saw just how much of her tanned legs showed beneath the scandalously short skirt or how sexy she felt in the crochet top. Would he remember the bathing suit?

"Thank you. I'm sorry you didn't call earlier, I would have liked going out for hamburgers," she said, holding on to the opened door, wishing he'd asked her last night, or at least had called this afternoon.

He shrugged, his eyes narrowing a bit. "I doubt it. I don't need fancy words for politeness' sake. You forget, I had a wife who lied at the drop of a hat. I'd much rather have the truth.''

Indignant, she drew herself up. "That was the truth. I think an evening with you would have been fun, unless you continued to attack my honesty. But Sally called and asked me to join them first."

He smiled sardonically at that. "And being the nicely brought-up young lady, you go with the first who invites you."

The sarcasm baffled her for a moment. Then she realized he didn't believe a word she'd said. Jackie probably discarded arrangements like old socks. But her mother had brought her up to honor commitments. While she had not called to confirm, neither had she called to cancel, so she knew they expected her.

A car turned into the driveway.

"Your date?" Cade asked, turning to watch the car approach.

"Just my ride. The designated driver." Wishing she'd called when she first arrived home and said she couldn't go, she was torn. An evening of fun beckoned, yet she really would have liked to spend the time with Cade.

Maybe it was better to go. She didn't want to become too dependent on Cade to provide her entertainment. She already wanted to spend all her time with him, better to pull back a little and hold on to her independence.

The driver stopped the car and stepped outside, calling over the top, "Hey, Jackie, ready to roll?"

"Be right there." Julianne retrieved her purse, checked to make sure she had her keys, and then closed the door. Cade had not moved. Suddenly she was almost pushing against him to get the door shut. His heat enveloped her, she could feel the warm cotton of his shirt against her shoulder.

"Your friend coming, too? It might be a tight squeeze," Toby asked.

She shook her head. "I'll see you tomorrow, then?" she asked Cade, sidestepping to put some distance between them.

"You can count on it." He pulled her up against him, pressed her mouth beneath his and kissed her hard. Releasing her, he cocked one eyebrow arrogantly and nodded. "Have fun tonight."

Julianne watched as he sauntered toward his home, stunned at the kiss, at her reaction. She couldn't believe he'd kissed her. Right in public, right with a carload of people watching. If she could get her breath, she'd yell after him and tell him—

"Jackie, let's go," Toby called.

She hurried the short distance to the car. Opening the back door, she slid into the seat next to Sally.

"Jackie, if you ever get tired of your neighbor, throw him my way. Wow, what a kiss, and you aren't even spending the evening with him. Didn't he want to come with?"

"Uh, I didn't ask him." She floundered, her pulse still beating lickety-split.

"Saving him for herself alone," another passenger murmured. "Jackie, how've you been? I'm glad Toby volunteered to drive. We're going to the Parkers's place first, then if that drags, we'll try Maggie's. I can't wait to get some dancing in. I haven't done anything physical in weeks."

"Yeah, if you don't count the swimming you're doing for that aquatics club," Sally said.

Julianne settled back and let the exchange wash over her.

Smiling, she tried to push Cade's audacious kiss from the forefront of her mind. She planned to memorize every moment of the evening. Gone was the uncertain librarian, in her place was wild and willing Jackie du Marcel. She would enjoy herself or die trying!

Cade watched the car turn and head down Jackie's driveway. Something didn't feel right, but he wasn't sure exactly what it was. She looked as sexy as hell, but he'd seen her look like that before. Tonight he'd been hard-pressed to keep casual when she'd opened the door. He had wanted to yank her inside, bolt the door behind them and kiss her until morning. Rubbing his fingers across his eyes, he tried to figure out this blatant attraction. It had more to do with the way she wore the clothes, maybe. That odd air of innocence that seemed to follow her. He didn't remember thinking that way about her before. Had the water in Italy mutated his brain cells?

When the car turned onto the street and sped away, he continued walking to his own patio. He loved the view of the ocean, loved the quiet and peacefulness he found in his home. Even though a short drive to L.A., he felt a million miles away when he was home.

Tonight the silence didn't bring the usual sense of peace. Dammit, he should have called her this afternoon and suggested dinner. He'd lived next door to her long enough to know she rarely stayed home alone. Jackie was a party girl, liked going places and seeing friends. She liked dancing, and laughing and seeing the bright lights. Nothing had changed in that. So why had he thought she would be waiting at home for him? Would be excited to go to dinner with him? She would see him tomorrow. She was free to do what she wished.

Of course tomorrow he had to share her with the others at the barbecue.

Share her? When did he want exclusivity with a woman? Not since the early days with Crystal. Hadn't he learned anything from that fiasco?

The evening loomed ahead, long and boring. How late would she stay out? How many different guys would she dance with? Kiss? Damn, he didn't care what she did. She was his next-door neighbor, nothing more.

The high-heeled sandals dangled from her fingers as Julianne inserted the key in the front door. When it opened, she turned and waved at the car. It sped away. Flipping on the inside lights, she closed the door behind her. The stairs seemed insurmountable. Dancing in high heels had been a mistake.

The shoes made her legs look long and curved, but they were awful for support. She'd finally kicked them off, but not until after she'd danced several hours wearing them.

"And I wish I had kept them on when that lecher at Maggie's tried his tricks. I could have stomped on his foot with the spike heel," she mumbled, pushing away from the door and limping toward the stairs.

On a scale from one to ten, she felt the evening was a definite nine or ten. She'd laughed, sampled Chinese and Mexican munchies, and danced so much she might never walk straight again. And more people kissed her than she even knew in Charlottesville. Some were friendly on-the-cheek greetings, several were on the lips, and one man, the lecher, had tried a bit more. If nothing else, it had proved how liked Jackie was among her friends.

Turning on the light in her bedroom, she switched off the hall light. Tossing the sandals in the direction of the closet, she headed for the bathroom. Maybe if she soaked her feet before going to bed they'd feel better in the morning.

The phone rang.

She stopped and stared at it. It was almost three o'clock in the morning, who could be calling her? It was too early for her mother, and too late for Jackie.

Limping across the room, she sank onto the bed and reached for the phone.

"Hello?"

"So if not dinner, how about breakfast?"

"Cade? Are you out of your mind? It's the middle of the night! You're calling me up to ask me out for breakfast?"

"Well, I was too late for dinner, so thought I'd get a start on breakfast."

"What are you doing up?" she asked suspiciously.

"Waiting to see what time you got home. Or if you even came home. Or if you came home alone."

Blinking, Julianne was speechless. How did she answer something like that?

"Of course I'd come home. Where else would I stay?"

"I'm not answering that question. Talk about a loaded gun."

Julianne leaned back on the bed and closed her eyes. She was so tired. "Thank you for the breakfast invitation, but I think it would have to be for lunch. I plan to sleep in until at least noon." She rotated her aching feet, even her ankles hurt.

"Then we'll make it brunch."

"Okay." She felt the urge to sleep pulling her. Could she muster enough energy to change into her nightshirt?

"Cupcake?"

Maybe she could just pull up the sheet and sleep in her clothes. There wasn't enough of them to be restrictive.

"Jackie!"

Julianne's eyes flew open. "What?" She'd drifted off. Sitting up, she shook her head. "I think I'm about to fall asleep. I'll see you tomorrow."

"I'll fix breakfast, okay?" Cade asked.

"Sure, whatever. Good night." She hung up, stripped off her top as she walked to the light switch. She shimmied out of her skirt in the dark and stumbled into the bed. In two seconds she was fast asleep.

The fragrant aroma of coffee wafted on the still air. Slowly Julianne turned over and drew a deep breath. Nothing smelled better than freshly brewed coffee early in the morning.

Coffee? She opened her eyes. The sun was already high in the cloudless blue sky, the room warmed from its rays. Slowly she sat up and sniffed. Coffee.

Cade had told her he would prepare breakfast. Had he meant in her own house? She threw off the covers and walked to her door, leaning against it to see if she could hear anything. The house seemed silent.

She reached for her robe and hesitated. Once before she'd gone downstairs in that terry-cloth robe, it was hardly her idea of glamour. Biting her lower lip in indecision, she considered the frothy nothings her sister had hanging in the closet. There was no way she could wear any of those if there was a man in the house!

Cade heard the shower. Good, she was up and he hadn't had to wake her. He glanced at the clock. How long did she take, a half hour, longer? He planned omelettes and toast. He could wait until she came down, as long as all the ingredients were ready. If she hurried, they could get in some beach time before they left for Phil's place.

"Now why did I think a breakfast invitation meant going out to eat somewhere, not providing the food myself?" she asked from the doorway.

Cade spun around. The shorts revealed long slender legs much as that sexy skirt had last night. The hot pink top added color to her cheeks. Her eyes were sparkling and fresh. He thought she looked good enough to eat.

"I'm cooking, that's something, right?"

"I guess." She stepped into the kitchen and looked around her with feigned surprise. "And are you a master chef?"

"Good enough for an omelette that you won't ever forget."

"The smell of the coffee woke me up."

"It's piping hot and ready to go." He poured her a cup and carried it to her. When she reached out to take the cup, he held it out of reach and leaned over. "Don't I get something for my efforts?" he asked, his lips hovering inches from hers.

"A nice 'thank-you'?" she asked, flirting.

"How nice?" he said softly.

"How nice do you want?" The throaty question pounded through his blood. She was an expert at this kind of thing, but he didn't mind. For a while, at least, she was his.

Her breath fanned across his face, minty and sweet. He wanted to taste her, see if she tasted like toothpaste.

"I could have made it breakfast in bed," he said, his eyes picking up the silvery shine in hers. Her lashes were long and curled, thick and dark.

"I already got dressed." Her breath came a bit faster, her eyes never left his.

Cade felt the pull of desire build. The enticing game drove him on.

"You could have stayed in bed."

"I wasn't dressed to receive company."

"If I were the company I wouldn't care. Did you sleep in your T-shirt?"

Slowly she shook her head, her mouth scant inches from his. He could cover the distance in a nanosecond, but he suddenly wanted her to come to him. If the banter was driving her as crazy as it drove him, she would have to give in soon.

"I was too tired last night. I took off my top and skirt and fell into bed." Her gaze dropped to his lips. When she promptly licked hers, he almost groaned aloud.

"In a lacy bra and skimpy panties?"

Julianne slowly smiled. If he knew she wore white cotton briefs and a serviceable bra, he'd probably burst out laughing. If he wanted to believe in the fantasy of sexy underwear, she would do nothing to disabuse him of the notion.

Her lips almost trembled in craving. His breath mingled with hers, his eyes so close she could see into their depths, deep green pools of mystery and adventure. Intrigued with the thought of kissing him, she leaned a bit closer. She could almost feel his lips against hers, could imagine the heat that would shimmer through her from him. Mesmerized by the challenge in his gaze, she moved a fraction closer still. She felt as if this man had cast a spell. Something propelled her along. She wanted desperately to feel those lips against hers. Wanted desperately to discover what his morning beard felt like against her cheeks. Wanted a taste of the most blatantly masculine, sexy adult male she'd ever met.

Forgetting the masquerade, forgetting twenty-four years of strict upbringing, almost forgetting her own name, she closed the distance—daring the fire that almost consumed her.

Julianne scarcely felt the touch of his lips before she wanted more. Taking a step closer brought her up against his hard body, between his muscular thighs. Heat flared when she felt the response from his mouth. She mimicked him, moving her lips, teasing with her tongue. Her heart pounded as desire kept her in place. Desire and curiosity. She wanted to see where this kiss would lead. It was not a soft brush of lips, but a full-blown, no-holds-barred, mouth-open kiss. Like the one on the patio had been. Like the ones in her dreams had been. On and on it went until she clutched his shoulders for support. Legs grown suddenly weak threatened to give way on her.

"Cupcake?" he questioned softly.

"You wanted a thank-you, right?" Julianne said, annoyed by the interruption. Was that husky tone hers? Where had this boldness come from? No time to analyze things. Julianne stood on tiptoes to better reach his mouth, rubbing her breasts against his chest as she strained to get closer. The moment her lips touched his again, he closed his eyes, and pulled her into his embrace, banding her with his strong arms, molding her softer body against his rock-hard frame. He opened her mouth and slowly, tantalizingly, let his tongue discover her taste, her feel, her sweetness.

Caught in the unexpected pleasure, her arms held as tightly as his. Stretched out against his body, she was surprised to find how right it felt, how much she wanted to stay just where she was forever.

She grew hot as the blood rushed through her veins. He tasted of coffee, sugar and tantalizing male heat.

She grew greedy as his kiss went beyond anything she'd experienced before. Julianne had no time to be shocked at her own unexpected wanton behavior, she was too busy exploring the sensations that exploded inside her. Feeling gloriously alive, her heart pounded in her chest, her breathing grew labored.

She yearned for more of the tingling feelings that shot through her in waves. She had never experienced such spine-shivering, wanton desire. She wanted more. For the first time she began to see what others found so alluring, so compelling. She never knew a single kiss could open her mind to the wild possibilities of a physical relationship between a man and a woman.

She'd never even come close with David.

The crash of breaking china, the splash of warm coffee against her leg had her springing back instantly.

"Jackie, are you hurt? You're not burned, are you?" Cade said, reaching out to her.

"No, I'm fine."

"Dammit." Cade looked at the broken cup. "I forgot I was holding it. Watch where you step, don't cut your foot." He lifted her out of the way of the shards of china and the spreading brown liquid.

Julianne stood where he placed her and watched him clean up the mess, gleefully recalling what he'd said. Becoming caught up in her kiss so much he'd forgotten he held the coffee? She must have been doing something right! So what if she didn't have the experience of her sister, she had mastered one aspect at least.

"Not a favorite cup, I hope," he said, stooping down to reach the coffee. Using a handful of paper towels, he mopped up the liquid and wiped up the china.

"No." Not of hers, anyway.

"Sit down and I'll fix breakfast as soon as I get this cleared up."

That was it? He kissed her like there was no tomorrow, now he says just sit down and he'll cook breakfast? Julianne limped stiffly to the table and gratefully sank onto the chair. Her lips were slightly swollen and warm. She licked them, tasting Cade. Her heart raced.

"Did you cut your foot?"

He stood, hands filled with dripping towels.

"No."

"You were limping."

"I'm sore from last night. I don't think I've ever danced so much. And the shoes I wore left a lot to be desired for comfort and support.'' She rotated her ankles, arching her aching feet.

"You still feel up to going this afternoon?"

"Of course, I'm looking forward to it." Julianne had enjoyed herself last night, but it had been a superficial kind of entertainment. She hadn't known any of the people and had bluffed her way through the entire evening without anyone suspecting she was not Jackie. Obviously they didn't know her sister very well, either. Was that how Jackie spent her life? In superficial activity, looking for good times and fun, rather than enjoying companionship with close friends? It didn't seem as appealing in the light of day.

She thought she could learn more about Cade at the barbecue, observing how his co-workers acted around him.

"There's no dancing, is there?" she asked.

"No. But we will—"

The phone rang, interrupting. Julianne almost let it go to the answering machine, but at the last ring she snatched it up. "Hello?"

"Hi, Julianne, it's Jackie. How are things going?"

Julianne's gaze swung around to Cade. Thank God, she'd answered before her twin's voice came across the answering machine. Fortunately he was engrossed in beating eggs in a large bowl. "Fine." If she pressed the receiver tightly against her ear, he would not be able to hear Jackie, would he?

"I didn't wake you up, did I?" Jackie asked.

"No. I'm up."

"My part is just about wrapped up. I told you it wasn't a big role. When I get the release, I'll hop on a jet and be home before you know it. Then we'll plan what to do to show you all around. Any ideas?"

"Uh, no, anything is fine."

Cade looked up. "Don't make plans," he whispered.

"What did you especially want to see when you thought about coming?" Jackie persisted.

"Nothing special." Julianne shook her head at Cade, wishing she dare put down the phone and take the call elsewhere. But she was afraid to remove the receiver from her ear.

"Julianne, is something wrong?"

"No."

Silence stretched out for several seconds.

"Are you alone?" Jackie's voice dropped several notches.

"No."

Jackie's laughter was soft. "I'm shocked. I thought you were the shy sister. You have some man in my house?" Jackie's voice held amusement and a hint of surprise.

"Yes," Julianne said, turning to look out the window.

"Let me guess, someone you met since you've been to California. It didn't sound like your dentist would chuck everything and follow you out."

"He's not *my* dentist anymore."

"Oh? My, my. That was fast. What happened?"

"It just wasn't right, I guess."

"If you can't talk, I understand, but I'll be home first chance I get. I want to hear all about this!" Jackie said.

"I'll see you then." Julianne slowly hung up, trying desperately to remember the gist of the conversation. She hadn't given anything away, had she? But the strain of the call played on her nerves. Slowly she turned to meet Cade's gaze.

"Who was that?" he asked.

"Someone who had a question about a dentist," she replied.

That was fast. What happened? her sister had asked. Cade happened, Julianne realized. And she didn't have a clue how to deal with it.

Eight

Julianne stared at Cade with new awareness. She had unconsciously used him as the role model for her ideal man. David couldn't compare, so she'd called to let him know she could never marry him. But neither could she marry Cade. He would never look twice at a mousy librarian who had grown up in a small Southern town. Surrounded by glamorous, successful women from the fast-paced world of L.A., why would he?

He's liked spending time with you since he returned from Italy, a small voice whispered.

He's liked being with the woman he thinks is Jackie, she replied firmly. She didn't believe in fooling herself. What would he do if she suddenly revealed herself, if she confessed to having lied to him for days?

She shuddered slightly and turned away. The masquerade had meant nothing, had simply been a lark, a blip in the greater scheme of things. She was attracted to him because he could kiss like no one else she'd ever met. And his looks were just short of perfect, but there were attractive men in Virginia. This attraction was a result of fantasy, of being on vacation. Day-to-day reality would not prove so romantic or compelling. He was just a man. Attraction could fade. She'd pull back, or something else would engage her attention.

"Here you go, one master omelette. It's got everything but the kitchen sink," Cade said, slipping a plate in front of her.

For a moment her resolve wavered. No one but her mother had ever fixed her breakfast. Maybe she should latch on to him and never let go. The eggs looked delicious. She cut into the steaming omelette, then tasted it.

"Wonderful," she said as the blend of flavors hit her tongue.

"My one major culinary accomplishment," Cade said smugly. In only moments he'd prepared one for himself and sat opposite her.

As they ate, conversation was sporadic. Julianne felt a comfortable ease between them that she'd not felt with any other man. Munching on toast, she gazed out the window, wondering at all the firsts. Was it an omen? Was Cade destined to be more than her sister's neighbor she met one vacation? Swinging her gaze to him, she watched as he ate, drank the coffee, slathered strawberry jam on his toast. What would it be like to share breakfast with him for all time? Would they discuss their day? Make plans for the future? Laugh at something the children had said?

Children? Carefully she laid the toast on the edge of the plate. She was getting a little carried away.

She'd just met the man a few days ago. And a wild attraction didn't necessarily mean anything. Hormones, chemistry. That's all. The fact that she found him fascinating proved how much she needed to experience life a bit more before settling down. He was outside her realm, and she was awed by their differences. Once she knew him better, he probably would become as predictable as David. Yet for the moment a rosy hue obscured that. To her, he was simply a totally foreign element to her normally staid existence.

"How did you get started in special effects?" she asked. There were probably three hundred questions she wanted answers for, but that one seemed the least revealing. She didn't want him to suspect her interest. Wouldn't that put him on his guard? Jackie had lived next door for two years yet had never mentioned him in any phone calls. Obviously she didn't see him in the same light as Julianne.

"I started out in animation. I liked cartoons as a kid, became interested in how they were done when I was in high school. My mother really pushed me to study so I could get a scholarship to the college of my choice. I was lucky to get into USC's film school. I began learning about animation, but once I discovered the amazing things that computers could do, I switched majors to computer science, and branched out from animation to special effects."

"And now you have your own company."

"Yeah, but it was a long time coming. I worked for some of the studios while in college and when I first graduated. When I scraped up enough money to buy some of my own equipment, I continued to do small jobs for the independents. I got a break when one of the major special effect studios couldn't take on a new film and the producer asked me. I came in on time and under budget and was the golden child for weeks. That led to more assignments, and finally I was able to open my own place."

"I'm impressed." Hollywood was a cutthroat business and to succeed as much as Cade had in so short a time was nothing short of phenomenal. Yet to talk to him, she would never have suspected. He exhibited none of the bragging or concentration on his own achievements that her father had displayed in their short lunch.

"So now you're rich and famous and doing what you like."

"I've got enough money to live here. Fame is fleeting, I just want the studios to know that they can count on my work. But you're right in that I'm doing just what I like. Aren't you?"

She thought of her job at the library. She enjoyed working with the patrons, researching hard-to-find tidbits of information, and being surrounded by books. Reading was her greatest pleasure, and to combine it with her job gave her a lot of joy.

"Yes, I love what I do," she said, finishing the last of the omelette.

"Playing the field and lying on the beach," he murmured.

She looked up at that. "Do I detect a note of censure?" she asked. For a moment she forgot she was in the role of her sister. She almost told him how hard she'd worked to get her current position.

"Not if doing nothing brings you happiness."

"You think I should be doing more?"

"What do you think?"

"I know what I think, I want to know what you think."

"Do what bring you happiness, cupcake. I learned that from my mother. She is one of the world's happiest people. If you look at material things, she doesn't have half as much as you or I. Yet she has a ton of friends, and really enjoys her life."

Julianne stared at him. There was more, she was sure. She had definitely detected disapproval in his comment.

Cade sighed softly and reached out for her hand, as if to anchor her against the words he planned to say.

"You're bright and pretty. You have a lot on the ball. I just think frittering your life away in parties and lazing around the beach is a waste of what brains you have. And I question how happy you are if you constantly need to seek activity, action. Do you find satisfaction from the roles you act in?"

"If I didn't, I wouldn't keep doing them," Julianne said, wondering if the reason Jackie was always on the move was because of dissatisfaction with her life. It was sobering. She'd always pictured Jackie as being blissfully happy. Julianne had always thought it would be wonderful to fly to the Riviera, or Paris, then back to California. Now Cade put doubts in her mind.

He squeezed her fingers and released her. "What do you want to do today?"

Learn more about you, she almost said. "Lie on the beach until it's time to get ready for the barbecue. What about you?" Her feet were still sore from all the dancing she'd done last night. The thought of doing nothing seemed perfect.

"Sounds good to me. I think we've finally finished with the Italians. Pete left last night to return home. I can just veg out and enjoy the day."

Southern California had a lot to offer, Julianne thought a little later as she spread sunscreen on her legs. The sky remained cloudless, the air warm against her skin. The quiet soughing of the surf provided a melodic background to the peaceful setting. The raucous crying of the gulls the only harsh note in a pristine day.

They did not have the beach to themselves. Two families had staked spots farther south, and the sound of children's laughter swept their way from time to time. Once, a dog barked.

"Want some?" she asked Cade, holding up the sunscreen bottle. He was already reclined on a towel, his body gleaming with a sheen of perspiration, muscles sculpted, belly flat. She kept her eyes resolutely above the brief bathing trunks he wore, which so clearly defined his masculinity.

"Not just yet. I put some on at home."

"Tell me more about the people I'll meet today," she said as she lay beside him and closed her eyes. The warmth of the sun soon had her floating. With the mesmerizing cadence of the surf and the low tone of his voice, she smiled. It was as perfect as things got. For a moment she imagined it was a typical day. They'd stay on the beach, go up for lunch, and maybe a nap—

Oops, maybe not. She concentrated on the descriptions he briefly sketched. At least he didn't expect her to know these people.

They talked, swam, shifted positions and dozed. A lazy day, Julianne conceded at one point, perfect for vacation. If she had been home, she would have risen early to dust and vacuum her apartment, done weekly chores and stopped by her folks' house to visit. Maybe she would have squeezed in a game of tennis or taken the kids to the pool. Then dinner with David, or a pleasant evening at friends or the show.

Instead she was free of chores and errands. With no friends demanding her attention, she could spend her entire day with Cade, reveling in each moment. Saving memories to take out later and enjoy a second time. A magical day.

Even the drive to the San Fernando Valley later seemed magical. As they left the beach behind, Julianne saw mountains in the distance. The infamous L.A. smog seemed to be missing as they drew closer. Crystal clear and soaring, the mountains provided a green backdrop, the soaring evergreens appearing to puncture the sky. Curious about the mountains, Julianne refrained from asking. Jackie undoubtedly knew, having grown up here.

The long driveway leading up to the huge house was crowded with cars when they arrived. Cade slipped the Porsche into a slot not too far from the house. As they walked to the front door Julianne noticed the air seemed warmer than at the beach. He pushed the doorbell. The noise inside and drifting around from the back virtually assured no one would hear the chimes. Opening the door, Cade motioned for Julianne to precede him.

She stepped inside, looking around at the eclectic array of furniture and paintings. Traditional and Early American blended with chrome-and-leather modern. The pictures on the walls ranged from what looked like a kindergartner's first rendition to a fine reproduction of a Monet. It was only a quick impression, however, for she was immediately enveloped in a bear hug by a huge, shaggy man.

"Hello, beautiful woman. I knew you would come into my life someday."

"Knock it off, Phil. The lady's taken," Cade said.

The man stepped back in surprise. "Taken? By who? You?"

"You have a problem with that?" Cade asked easily. He pulled Julianne closer, encircling her shoulders with one arm in a decidedly masculine staking of a claim.

Phil shook his blond head, the long strands swaying in tempo. "Just never figured it." Turning to Julianne, he smiled. "Welcome, fair lady. I'm Phil Mott."

"How do you do? I'm Jul—Jackie du Marcel." Her hand was instantly engulfed in his.

"And do you admit to being Cade's lady?" he asked, leaning a bit closer, his voice lowered, intimate—as if Cade wasn't standing two inches away. She smiled.

"I came with him."

"Not at all the same thing!" he said in triumph, glancing at Cade.

"The same thing. Where's the bar?" Cade growled.

Julianne tilted her head to look at him. Was he jealous? It was so obvious that Phil was the kind of guy to kid everyone. She was intrigued with Cade's frown. Surely he knew Phil was teasing. Was his reaction an act?

"The bar is on the deck. We've already started cooking, so help yourself when you want to eat. This is catch as catch can. Enjoy. I'll catch up with you later." Phil patted Julianne on the shoulder and gave her a wink. With a wide grin at Cade, he moved on.

"Want something to drink?" Cade asked. His hand slid to the small of her back and he gently guided her through the clusters of people until they reached the huge wooden deck. Steps led to the yard, a huge free-form pool to the left. To the right several huge barbecue grills had been set up. The tantalizing aroma of ribs and chicken smothered in rich sauce wafted in the air.

Julianne felt her mouth water. She saw several people seated on scattered tables near the pool, platters of ribs piled in front of them.

"I'd like a glass of white wine," she said. "And then something to eat. My mouth is watering."

"Jackie!" A pretty red-haired woman pushed through another couple and, smiling broadly, came up to Julianne. Giving her a big hug, she stepped back. "I didn't know you were coming. In fact I heard you'd gone to Mexico to film your part early. How have you been? We have to get together soon and catch up on all the news!"

"That'd be great. Why don't you call me?" Julianne hoped desperately she wouldn't be called on to introduce this woman to Cade.

"Let's just say Tuesday. At twelve-thirty? Want to come to my place? I'll fix shrimp salad."

"Mmm." Who was this woman, and where did she live? Julianne couldn't agree, she hadn't a clue.

"Hello, Margot," Cade said, returning with two glasses in hand. He handed one to Julianne.

"Cade, hi!" Glancing from one to the other, Margot's eyebrows rose. "Are you two dating?"

"Cade brought me here," Julianne said, wondering if that counted as a date.

"Ah," Margot nodded, her eyes dancing. "Now I insist on lunch Tuesday, you have more to tell me than I have to tell you."

"I'll have to get back to you," Julianne said vaguely.

"Sure, whatever. Call me tomorrow. In the meantime, did you know Batts is dating Nigel? I heard it from Richard. I can't believe it myself, but you know Richard."

Julianne sipped her wine and nodded, totally lost to the conversation. Was she going to be exposed at the onset that she was not Jackie? Could she impersonate her sister for the duration of the party? Glancing at Cade, she noticed he appeared bored with the trend of the conversation. Not that she blamed him. She wasn't one to gossip about others, especially when she didn't even know the people.

"Hi, Cade, good to see you." A pretty dark-haired woman linked her arm with his and leaned against him casually. Her skirt was short, her halter top cut to reveal the charms she so artlessly displayed.

Julianne wanted to knock her arm away and let her know loud and clear that Cade was her date for the evening. Shocked at her primitive thoughts, she took another sip of wine and tried to calm down. She had never felt so strongly before, even when she and David had been dating for several months.

Of course, she never felt for David what she felt for Cade. Oh, God. No!

She was falling in love with her sister's neighbor! The knowledge struck her instantly as everything fell into place. Her attraction to him, her sudden certainty she and David would never work, her dreams at the breakfast table, lying on the beach. She was falling in love with Cade Marshall! Panic set in. She wanted to run as far and as fast as she could. Trapped at this party, she felt helpless. Her mind spun, her thoughts in turmoil. What was she thinking of, falling for the man? He ate women like her up for lunch.

"Hi, Shelley. Have you met Jackie du Marcel? She's my next-door neighbor," Cade said easily. "I think you already know Margot Porter."

Shelley nodded at Margot, then swung her gaze at Julianne. Her eyes narrowed briefly, then an insincere smile turned up her lips. "Nice to meet you."

Julianne shivered. If looks could injure, she'd be picking herself up off the floor right now. The lovely Shelley must have a particular interest in Cade. One that was not returned? Jealousy speared again. She sure hoped it wasn't returned!

"So you already know some people," Phil said, joining them, his smile directed straight at Julianne.

"Just met Shelley," she murmured. Looking at the woman, she asked, "Do you work at Cade's place, also?"

"Yes, production manager."

Julianne swung back to Phil. "And what do you do?"

"Chief dreamer, right, boss?"

"After me," Cade said.

"Dreamer?" Julianne asked.

"I dream up the stuff. Sometimes the script calls for some sort of special effect we haven't tried before. I dream up how to map it out to get the most realism from the scene, then block it out on the computer. And Cade's right, he does it more than me. Funny, isn't it?"

"What?" Julianne asked.

"How a guy who is so adamantly against liars is such a liar himself." Phil laughed when he looked at Cade.

"I don't equate the two," Cade replied easily.

"I know, but when you think about it, that's what we do. Sell lies to people."

"Special effects are created from fiction, hardly the same thing as a lie."

"Isn't fiction one big lie?" Phil persisted.

"Most people can differentiate between a fictitious piece of work and a lie between friends or acquaintances," Cade said.

"Or spouses," Phil added slyly.

Cade nodded, his face stiff and expressionless.

Julianne wanted to defuse the tension that sparked between the two men, and escape from Cade for a few minutes. She needed some time to come to terms with her startling discovery.

"I'm hungry." She looked at the barbecue grills, the tantalizing aroma causing her mouth to water. Phil took her arm and turned her toward the grills.

"Come with me, pretty lady, and I'll see you have more food than you can possibly eat."

Cade said nothing, so Julianne went meekly with Phil. At least peace was restored.

"Cade's okay," Phil said as they waited behind another couple to be served.

"From your discussion, I might have guessed you didn't like him."

"Hey, I think he's great. He's smart as a whip, really can do the most fantastic stuff with software, and he's easy to work for."

"Weren't you pushing a bit about the lies?" she asked quietly.

"Yes, maybe. I rag on him a bit because he's so inflexible. Because of his wife, of course."

"She told lies," Julianne said.

"Whoppers. Of course he has a bit of a strong moral backbone anyway, but Crystal really did a number on him. So now he tries to bend over the other way. Very intolerant about some things now. And he never tells even the smallest untruth that I've ever discovered."

"Most people don't." Most people didn't impersonate their sisters, lie to everyone they met during the past week about whom they were. Guilt stole over her, heat colored her cheeks. She'd been living a lie. What had started out as merely a fun idea had now blown all out of proportion. And the worst of it was, she was falling in love with a man who was highly intolerant of deception and liars.

"Here we go. What's your pleasure?" Phil handed her a plate. When both their plates had been piled high with barbecued chicken, he nodded to a quiet table near the pool. "Want to sit while we eat?" he asked.

"Sure." She glanced back at Cade. He appeared in deep conversation with two other men. Shelley still hung on to his arm. Julianne followed Phil to the empty table and sat down. The water reflected the late afternoon sun. The murmur of voices sounded quite different from the soft crash of waves from the sea. Pretty soon she'd return home, hundreds of miles inland, away from the sea and the feeling of being on the edge of the world. And away from parties like this one.

Julianne stared at Phil. His shaggy blond hair made him look as if he were a surfer rather than a highly skilled com-

puter programmer. His tan proved he spent a lot of time outdoors. When did he work, at night?

"Do you always cut away your friends' dates?" she teased.

"Do you always go?"

She shook her head, then glanced involuntarily at Cade, her
smile fading a bit. "No, but I don't think he'll miss me."

"Shows how much you know, or how little. This is the first
time he's brought someone to one of our parties. Cade has
been a cagey man ever since he dumped Crystal. I find it very
interesting that he brought you today."

"He doesn't date?" she asked, finding that almost impossible to believe.

"Of course he dates, he's a man, isn't he? But there are
dates and dates. The ones he usually goes on do not involve
friends. He takes a woman to dinner or a movie or dancing,
but it is strictly one-on-one, and he doesn't mingle those
women with his friends. Especially not the friends he works
with. You're the first since Crystal."

"So you knew Crystal?" she asked.

"Yes, still do, as a matter of fact. I see her from time to
time. That's the other thing. You are even more beautiful than
Crystal. From the few women I've caught Cade with over the
last three years, I thought he only picked out the ones who
were not especially beautiful—a backlash, if you would, from
Crystal. Another exception with you."

"I'm not beautiful," she protested. Granted, her mother often said she looked pretty, but mothers were supposed to say
so.

Phil put down the drumstick he'd almost bitten, staring at
her. "I think you believe that," he said in wonder.

"I'm not beautiful." Julianne was definite on that point.
Maybe the clothes changed things a bit. They were daring and
glamorous and colorful. Her usual pick of pastels and neutral
tones had given way to Jackie's flamboyant selections. That's
what Phil saw, and maybe Cade? He would probably not look
twice at a woman who normally dressed in beige and tan.

"Now I get it," he said mysteriously.

"Get what?" she asked warily as she ate the succulent chicken.

"The attraction. A beautiful woman who doesn't know she's beautiful. And I'll bet you are not impressed with material things."

"Like what?"

"You know, a house in Malibu, a Porsche."

"I'm living in a house in Malibu."

"Do you like it?"

"Yes."

"Are you so impressed by your address you mention it to all who come in contact with you?" he persisted. "I mean, I was the one who brought it up just now."

"Of course not. It's just a house on the beach."

"Cade's that way. He bought the house because he wanted to live at the beach, and liked the architecture. I think he bought his car to get back at Crystal."

"You're kidding."

Phil shook his head, taking a huge bite from a drumstick. "Nope. Does he strike you as car mad? I have friends who have fancy cars, and brag about them all the time, telling me how fast they go, or how many women's heads they turn on the highway. The common theme is they constantly talk about their car. Cade never mentions his. I think he bought it solely to get back at Crystal. She loves flashy symbols of affluence."

"Oh." She thought about her brothers. They fit the role Phil had described, talking about torque and RPMs and all sorts of things that weren't a bit of interest to her. Cade had never said a word about his car.

"I take it this is not a private party," Cade said, placing a plate on the table.

Julianne looked up and smiled, shaking her head. "I couldn't wait to eat, though. We didn't have lunch, and breakfast was a long time ago."

Phil's eyes gleamed at her remark. "Maybe I'm the one crashing a private party," he said.

Cade dragged a chair over and sat down, his knee brushing against Julianne's, resting against her leg. "We'll just leave if it comes to that," he said.

Phil laughed. "Where did you find this treasure?" he asked.

"Right under my nose. Jackie has the house next door."

"Ah, no wonder she's not so impressed with your wealth."

"Phil." There was a warning edge in Cade's tone.

"I was just about to ask Jackie for her life's story."

"You don't want to hear it," she replied. "I'd much rather hear about your firm, how you get contracts, how you decide what you will do for special effects, what works, what problems you've had, things like that. I know about me, I don't have a clue about what you do."

"Cade can go on all night if you get him started, so be careful what you ask for," Phil said. When a newly arrived couple paused on the steps, he rose. "Duty calls. I'll get back when I can. In the meantime, Cade, be sure to give credit where it's due." With that parting comment, Phil shot across the patio to greet the newcomers.

"He's funny," Julianne said, her eyes following him.

"He's also brilliant. Though I don't tell him often. He has a healthy ego and I don't need to feed it to make it any larger."

"He says you have the real brains in the company."

"Politically correct to the end. I am the boss."

"Somehow I don't think he'd say that if it weren't true. He also considers himself a friend of yours and vice versa."

"That's right." Cade began to eat. "Why not?"

While Julianne was on a cordial basis with her own boss, they were too far apart in experience, and age, to be friends. And they kept the chain of command very strict at the library. The friendship between Cade and his employees struck her as unusual. She shrugged. "Nothing's wrong with it. In fact, it sounds nice. But it's a bit unusual, don't you think?"

"No. It's the way I wanted to run a company. We work together, sometimes days and nights if we get behind. If we didn't like each other and respect each other, it'd be hell."

"I bet you are a stickler."

"I have high standards, and expect everyone else to stick to them. Nothing I wouldn't do myself."

"And is your dislike for liars part of your high standards?" she asked slowly.

"Doesn't everyone dislike being lied to?" he countered.

She nodded, and let her gaze drift over the pool. How would she feel if she found that he'd been lying to her? That he wasn't who she thought he was, that it had been a game? Would she understand, or be incredibly hurt when she discovered the truth?

Nine

Suddenly the masquerade lost its appeal. Where she had been enjoying herself, now she felt a fraud. Glancing around at the laughing groups, talking and sharing an evening together, she felt guilty that she'd come in false pretenses. Turning slightly, she angled her chair away from Cade. How could she have let the impersonation continue for so long? It was one thing for him to mistake her at breakfast that first morning, and a lark to see if she could come across as her sister. But she should have cleared things up instantly. Or at their next meeting.

How could she make things right?

It was obvious she had to tell him, confess her foolishness and pray he'd understand. But what if he didn't? Fear clamped down on her. If he didn't, he'd walk away and never look back. And she wasn't sure she could take that right now, not moments after realizing she was falling in love.

She had no clue to his feelings. Granted he spent time with her. They seemed to click on all levels. He had kissed her, caressed her, and she suspected would have pursued the encounter a lot further if she'd been more receptive. How would she find a way to tell him so he'd understand? She hadn't meant to go so far with the charade. She'd only wanted to find a bit of the magic she always associated with her sister.

Before she could think more about the awkward situation she'd put herself into, before she could devise a way to extricate herself, another couple joined them at the table. From that point until it was time to leave, Julianne didn't have a moment to herself.

She laughed at the jokes, and murmured soft replies when asked direct questions. Trying to place names with faces, she studied each person she met. Throughout the evening, Cade never strayed more than a step away. He rested his hand on her shoulder, or pulled her close a time or two in a brief hug. Once he'd linked his fingers with hers, swinging their hands between them casually as he listened to one of the men give a detailed description of some golf tournament he'd won.

As the evening progressed, she grew more and more attuned to Cade. Her body felt as if it walked a tightrope strung far above the ground. One misstep and she'd crash. Awareness shimmered through her, and every touch he made notched up the level. She wished the others would fade away and leave Cade alone with her beneath the dark night sky.

"Ready to go home?" he asked after checking his watch.

"So soon?" Phil protested. "It's hardly midnight."

"It's after one and we have a long drive," Cade said, linking his fingers with Julianne's again.

"I didn't realize it was so late, I am tired," she said. Truth to tell, she couldn't wait to be alone with Cade. The party had been wonderful, fulfilling every dream she'd had of the exciting glamorous life she imagined Jackie took for granted. But the more the evening wore on, the more she wished to be alone with Cade. Maybe he'd kiss her again, hold her. Or they could just talk as they drove home. Somehow she had to find a way to tell him who she was, and make him understand why she'd played such a foolish trick.

The Porsche was a cozy cocoon as Cade drove swiftly, competently, through the dark streets leading to the freeway.

"I enjoyed meeting so many of your friends," she said when the lights of the houses had been left behind.

"They're all good people."

"And funny, especially Jim and Phil."

"Jim's our resident clown. No matter how tense a situation can get, he comes up with some joke that eases the mood."

"His wife is very pretty."

"So are you."

Julianne stared at him, seeing the soft glow from the dashboard illuminate part of his face. He seemed serious. He looked over at her, back to the road.

"What changed while I was in Italy?" he asked.

"I don't know what you mean." She swallowed hard. Chalk up another lie.

"We've known each other for two years, and yet there's something different about you. Or maybe it's different about me. I noticed it as soon as I returned from Italy, this attraction between us. It was never there before, was it?"

Julianne swallowed. So he hadn't been attracted to Jackie. A huge weight seemed to roll off her shoulders. The attraction wasn't one-sided, and while he didn't know yet she was not Jackie, he had never been attracted to Jackie. Maybe when she told him why she'd pretended to be someone she was not, he'd forgive and forget.

"And don't play innocent about what attraction I'm talking about."

"I'm not," she said quietly, her heart racing. How did she handle this?

"So where do we go from here?" he asked.

"Where do you want to go?" Panic set in. What if he wanted more than she could offer? What if it was just a lark to him, as impersonating Jackie had started out for her?

"For starters, I thought you could spend the night."

She swallowed and gazed blindly out the windshield. Here

it was, laid out plain for her to say yes or no. And she wanted
to say yes. She had waited all her life to experience this glow
of love and enchantment that enveloped her. Could she risk
everything and say yes? To spend the night with Cade, to love
him, sleep with him, and wake up together in the morning?

Nervously she rubbed her damp palms against her skirt. She
was so unsure and inept at this.

When his warm hand enveloped one of her hands, she jumped.
He brought their hands to rest on his thigh. "Say yes, cupcake."

"I'm just not sure." Her heart melted at the endearment.
She felt cherished and special that he had a pet name for her.
David always called her Julianne. Only her family ever short-
ened it.

"About what?"

"Us, you and me. This. It seems so monumental. And we
haven't known each other very long." Was it less than a
week?

"Two years is a long time. I see your staying over as the
next logical step in our relationship," Cade said. "I know
what I want. If you want the same thing, what's the problem?"

"Well, for one thing, you don't know about me."

"I know all I need to know. I've felt this attraction since
you came downstairs in that terry-cloth robe and fixed me
French toast. Being with you this week has strengthened that
attraction."

"You say we've known each other for two years, but not
well. I mean—"

"I know all I need to know about you. Tonight you met a
few of my friends, I met some of yours at that party last fall.
We've talked a lot over the last week, actually spent more
time together since I returned from Italy than over the past
two years."

"No, you think you know me, but actually—"

"Actually it doesn't matter. Just say yes."

"I need to tell you something first," Julianne said, her heart beating so heavily she could scarcely breathe. Once he heard her confession, would he dump her out of the car? Yell at her for her lies?

He smiled and squeezed her hand slightly. "You think you are falling in love with me."

Her eyes widened in astonishment. Had she been that obvious?

Cade looked at her, then back to the road. "Right?"

"Am I that obvious?"

"No, but maybe I'm falling in love with you. Maybe we can see and feel that emotion in each other."

She sat back, bewildered. Was he really falling in love with her? Or was it some line sophisticated men used to lure unsuspecting, gullible women into their lair? If he truly loved her, wouldn't he have said something earlier? Why now, when he was pushing to get her into bed. She wanted it to be true, but was too unversed in the entire scene to trust her instincts.

"Okay, baby, forget it. Stop in for a brief nightcap and head for your chaste little bed," Cade said sharply.

Did she detect anger, or disappointment? Julianne wasn't sure, but she was sure she felt like an idiot. She loved this man. He had practically admitted he loved her in return. And if Phil's comments were anything to go by, it was highly unusual for Cade to be so demonstrative with women.

"Tell me about Crystal," she said unexpectedly.

"Not tonight. What I want has nothing to do with Crystal. She is ancient history. You've noticed I never asked about your husband."

She'd never had a husband. Oh, Jackie. "Cade, I have to tell you—"

"No, you don't have to tell me anything tonight. Have a drink and go home," he repeated.

Julianne lapsed into silence. The miles sped by as he drove west toward the beach. She grew sleepy and had a hard time staying awake. Her thoughts should have been enough to insure she never slept again, but tired from the night before, the day at the beach and the lateness of the hour, her eyes felt dry and could hardly stay open.

"A drink?" Cade asked as he turned onto their street.

"A quick one, maybe," she said. Tired or not, she was not ready for the evening to end.

Turning on a single lamp in his living room, Cade went to the bar installed along a portion of the glass wall and poured two small brandies. Julianne wandered to the window that overlooked the ocean and gazed out at the dark expanse. Stars scattered in the sky gave a soft radiance, overwhelmed by the brightness of the moonlight. Silvery waves moved as far as she could see, almost as if they provided a path straight to heaven.

"It's so pretty here," she said when he offered her the brandy snifter.

"That's why we live here, I guess."

What would it be like to live here, to have the ocean as a presence in her life? To hear the waves endlessly kiss the shore, to feel the clear breeze against her skin, to become used to the slightly tangy salt air? She loved it here and wished she could stay forever. Even though home beckoned, there was something special about this place.

When Cade took her untouched glass, she didn't resist. When he leaned over and kissed her, she opened her lips and closed her eyes to better experience the kiss. His arms brought her up against his strength and molded her softer body against his hard one. Deepening the kiss, he gave her no time to think. She could only feel the exquisite sensations that pulsed through her with his touch. Her arms encircled his neck and she pressed herself wantonly against him. Feeling daring and brave, she threaded her fingers in his thick hair and responded to the passion that clamored to be released.

When his lips left hers to trail damp kisses across her cheek, down her neck, she shivered. But was it heat or cold that trapped her body? Icy fire trails followed his every caress and Julianne followed each touch in her mind. Her hands kneaded his shoulders, moved to trace the strong line of his chest. His followed a like trail, coming around to cup one full breast and massage gently.

When his thumb flicked across her aroused nipple, the thrill went straight to her center. She felt warm and cherished, hot and bothered, and craved more touch than a soft caress through her dress.

"Stay," Cade whispered in her ear, his tongue tracing the outline, his breath causing shivers of delight.

"Yes," she replied, knowing she had wanted to acquiesce all along. What held her back? Slowly she turned her face and found his, staring deeply into his green eyes, wishing the light was off and they could see by moonlight.

His lips found hers again and he kissed her long and hard.

"Are you sure, sweetheart?" he asked, pulling back just enough to see her.

"Yes," she said again, giving in to the wave of love that swept through her. She had lived twenty-four years and never felt like this before. She hadn't known what pleasure her body could tune in to, hadn't known the touch of a man's hand could bring such delight.

Cade kissed her gently and began to move them toward the hallway, as if dancing to a slow, soft melody. His hands ignited her, leaving fire in their wake. His kisses inflamed her, causing her temperature to skyrocket.

Julianne kissed him deeply, daringly letting her tongue entice him, tease him, dance with his. Her hands savored the feel of the strong muscles of his arms and chest. His back was broad, and her fingers learned his shape as his muscles moved.

She was almost shocked when they stopped. The bedroom was illuminated by the silvery glow of the moon. Mysterious shadows danced on the edge of the light, the bed stood right beside them.

Cade's knowing fingers quickly found the fastenings of her dress, released them and pushed the material from her shoulders. As it slid along her skin, Julianne realized even the brush of cloth heightened her sensitivity. She was more alive than ever, and every bit of her focused on Cade Marshall.

Fumbling with inexperience, she unfastened the buttons on his shirt, her fingers tangling between the material and his chest, feeling the brush of hair, the heat of his skin. She grew impatient, wanting to rip the shirt from his shoulders. How many buttons did the blasted shirt have?

"Easy, baby, we have all night," Cade whispered against her skin as she yanked at the offending shirt.

"I want you now," she complained.

His teeth gleamed in the dim light as he smiled at her tone.

"I want you right now, too, Miss Impatience," he said.

In only seconds their clothes had been discarded and Cade lifted her to place her in the center of the large bed. He came down beside her instantly, his mouth finding hers, his hand moving against her shoulder, down one arm, and across to her belly. Slowly, agonizingly slowly, he moved up until he touched her breast.

Julianne arched against his hand, conscious of the primal beat that pushed her closer and closer to that ultimate intimacy. She reveled in the discoveries as each unveiled itself. How hot his skin felt against her; how hard parts of his body seemed; how big and strong and sexy the man was. And how every touch evoked joy and delight and blazing passion.

Sleep was forgotten as exploration expanded. Touches and caresses and kisses had no boundaries—only the goal of providing pleasure. She learned his body as he learned hers, and she found passion grew with each moment.

By the time Cade came over her, Julianne was so hot she thought she would melt into the bed. Her body pulsed and ached and she knew something was missing, but couldn't find out what it was exactly.

"Don't leave," she cried when he moved away for a moment.

"I'm not leaving, just getting protection," he said, covering her in only seconds. His hot body felt like a heavy blanket, one she pulled close and encircled with her arms. When he tested her readiness, she pushed herself against him.

"More," she panted.

"Much more," he agreed. Pushing into her, Cade surged, only to be checked.

"What the hell?" He lifted himself away from her on strong arms, staring down into her face.

Julianne had not expected the tearing pain that accompanied his thrust. But it faded, and the reality of their situation paled beside the impossible urge to continue, to find that spark that had been so close.

"Don't stop," she implored him, shifting her hips, seeking something that she knew had to be near.

Cade kissed her, his body moving in a rhythm that grew stronger and faster by each second. When he thrust hard one last time, Julianne cried out as the rippling waves of exquisite pleasure poured through her body. He groaned and held himself rigid and she held on like she'd never let him go.

Gradually the high faded.

Gradually she cooled.

Gradually sleep claimed her.

Julianne shifted slowly, the sheet moving against her bare skin. Slowly she opened her eyes. The room was unfamiliar. Looking around, she caught her breath when she saw Cade asleep next to her. Memories of last night instantly crashed through her mind. They had made love. Her first time. Slowly she smiled as she studied the sleeping man. Somehow being asleep didn't soften the harsh lines of his face. She missed seeing his green eyes, however. Missed how they danced in amusement, or changed to a deeper mysterious green when he grew serious or angry.

She shifted, feeling aftereffects of their activity. Making love with the man she loved had to be heaven on earth. She wished he'd wake up and make love to her again.

Suddenly she remembered his reaction when he'd discovered she was a virgin. There would be questions galore this morning, she knew. How was she supposed to explain a husband? She should have insisted he listen last night. Should have told him the entire story, and explained about wanting to act like Jackie for a while.

Slipping from the bed, she looked for her clothes. The dress lay in a heap where she'd stepped out of it last night. She pulled it on. Panties were located where Cade had tossed them. She picked up her shoes and slowly left the room, quietly moving away lest she wake him.

Julianne didn't know what to do, but she knew she had to have some distance to decide. Guilt lay like a blanket over her shoulders. He would be furious if he discovered her deception before she could explain things to him. She needed to decide just how to do that.

She snatched her bag on her way through the living room and turned off the lamp that still shone. Letting herself out, she quickly ran across the dew-damp grass. Opening the kitchen door, she stopped suddenly.

"Wondered where you were," Jackie said, smiling broadly.

"Oh! Jackie, I didn't know you were coming home yesterday." Julianne carefully closed the door as pangs of embarrassment hit her. There could be no question in anyone's mind as to where she'd been or what she'd been doing. Her hair wasn't combed, her dress was wrinkled and only half-fastened, and she carried her shoes.

"Caught an earlier flight. Got here about nine last night. Gave up on you around eleven. Have fun?" Jackie asked, leaning against the counter and letting her gaze travel up and down her twin, teasing lights dancing in her eyes.

"Actually I did," Julianne said defiantly.

"I'm all for people having fun," Jackie said mildly. "Want some coffee, it's just brewed."

"Later. I need to change." Julianne held her head high as she walked through the kitchen. Of all times for her sister to return. Couldn't she have had at least one day to herself to sort through her emotions?

A half hour later Julianne entered the kitchen. She'd showered, washed her hair and dried it. The jeans and cotton shirt she wore were her own. No more pretending to be her sister, no more wearing Jackie's clothes. The faded light blue denim molded her figure like an old skin. The pink top was one of her favorites. She needed all the comfort she could get. No matter how many ways she'd thought of to tell Cade, they all sounded inadequate.

She felt comfortable, but not a bit glamorous. So much for living life as Cinderella. Now the pumpkin had returned and the slipper was lost. And some time today she had to tell Cade Marshall who she really was.

"I'll take that coffee now," she said as she headed for the counter.

Jackie sat at the table, lounging in one of her vividly colored silk jumpsuits—this one a hot teal, which glowed in the early morning sun. She waved her hand in the direction of the pot. "Help yourself. I had toast. If you want some you can help yourself to that, as well. Or we could go out for breakfast later. I like a big leisurely Sunday brunch. What do you think?"

"No, just coffee." The thought of food on an already churning stomach was more than she wanted to consider.

"So, want to talk about where you were?" Jackie asked when Julianne sat opposite her.

"Not especially." She sipped the hot beverage. Her nerves jangled. She probably should have had decaf.

"Anyone I know?" Jackie persisted, her eyes dancing in amusement.

The angry knock caught Julianne off guard. Stunned, she turned toward the door. She knew who was pounding, and she wasn't ready!

Jackie unwound from the chair like a slinky cat. She crossed the kitchen floor as if she glided, and threw open the door. If she were surprised to see Cade standing there almost breathing fire, she hid it well.

"Listen, lady, when you stay the night—" Cade caught sight of Julianne and stopped dead. Narrowing his gaze, he looked at Jackie, back at Julianne.

"Dammit, I *knew* there was something—"

"Want to come in for coffee?" Jackie asked.

He pushed past Jackie and stormed across the kitchen, green fire blazing in his eyes. Reaching out, a hard hand grasped Julianne's arm and half lifted her from the chair.

"I want to talk to you," he snarled, turning and heading for the door, pulling her beside him, ignoring Jackie.

"Cade—" Jackie started.

"Not now." He continued out the door and across the yard toward the boundary line between the two houses.

Julianne almost ran to keep up with him. "Where are we going?" she asked.

He stopped abruptly and swung her around, glaring at her. His breath came fast, his hand tightened on the soft flesh of her upper arm. For a moment the only sound was the muffled crash of waves on the beach beyond the edge of the bluff.

"Hell, if I know. Not to my house, that's for sure. Dammit, I should have suspected something, but I never knew you— Jackie had a *twin* sister. What was your game? God, I don't even know who you are!"

She cleared her throat; tried to push away the fear that crowded. "I'm Julianne Bennet, Jackie's sister."

"I can see you're sisters, you're *twins!*"

She nodded. "I'm sorry. Cade, listen to me."

"And you should be damned sorry. I was falling for you!" He released her arm and spun around, taking several steps toward the edge of the cliff, his hands clinching into fists. "I should have known better. *Dammit!*" He kicked a tuft of grass.

"I didn't mean any harm," Julianne said, stepping closer. "Truly. If you would listen, I can explain."

He looked over his shoulder. "Like hell." His eyes scanned her from head to toe. Shaking his head, he half turned. "It's my fault. I've known your sister for two years. The minute I saw the terry robe I should have known it wasn't Jackie. I didn't know her well, but every indication pointed to her being like Crystal. Once she had fancy clothes, the mundane would not suit."

"I can explain," Julianne repeated.

"Go for it."

She took a deep breath. "I didn't start out pretending to be Jackie. I was surprised when you thought I was her. I mean, I'm hardly the glamorous twin. I haven't led an exciting life. Living in a small town with my family, visiting California is probably the most exciting thing I'll ever do. But you thought I was Jackie. And I've always thought she led such a charmed life, I just gave in to a silly impulse and didn't correct you. I mean, you can't imagine the lift that gave me. For once someone thought I was glamorous, exciting." She trailed off as she realized his expression hadn't softened.

He looked away, the muscles in his cheek jumping as he clenched his jaw.

She had to try. "I was caught up in the fantasy. She left almost as soon as I arrived. Jackie even suggested I try on her clothes, drive her car. It was fun, playing like these things were mine, like I fit into the California life-style. When I met you, I couldn't believe you'd give me the time of day, much less spend so much time with me."

"My wife lied to me," he said in a low, hard voice. "She cheated behind my back, and fed me a host of lies. I swore I would never again be taken in by another woman."

"I didn't start out to fool you, you mistook me for Jackie. And I thought it so fantastic, I just played along for a little while. Then time went on and still I pretended. When I realized that—" Julianne stopped. She dare not mention falling in love, he would scoff at her tender emotion. "I tried to tell you last night in the car. Twice. But both times you said not to talk. I had no idea we would end up in bed."

"You could have said something. I've thought I was losing

my mind. I do not like what your sister stands for, she's too much of a reminder of Crystal. But there was something different when I got back from Italy.'' He ran a hand through his hair.

Julianne wanted to brush down his hair, push back the lock that fell over his forehead. He hadn't shaved. Had he awakened and immediately come after her? Had she ruined everything by her masquerade?

"I'm sorry, Cade. I didn't mean to hurt you."

His look caused her to step back. Blazing anger met her gaze. "I'm not *hurt*, Julianne Bennet. Mad as hell that I fell for another woman's lies, but not *hurt*. You have to care about somebody before they can hurt you." He strode away without another look. In seconds she heard the slamming of his door. Then the soft sound of the sea drifted up from the beach. Other than that, it was silent.

Julianne watched him walk away, shocked at the turn of events. Words crowded her mind. She had to explain. Slowly she followed. When she reached the heavy wooden door of his Spanish-style house, she still hadn't decided exactly what to say, but somehow she had to make him see she was not like Crystal, that she had not meant to deliberately lie, only been caught up in the masquerade.

Yet she had, maybe not with any malicious intent, but she'd lied nonetheless.

She knocked. Waited. Nothing. There was silence behind the door.

"Cade, please, give me a couple of minutes." She rapped again. Her knuckles hurt. She opened her hand and pounded her palm against the unforgiving door. Only silence met her efforts.

Slowly she turned and walked away. Tears threatened and she blinked rapidly. She could not give way to tears, she had to think. Last night had been wonderful, perfect. Would he ever even listen to her, let her atone for fooling him? Would they have other nights where they could kiss and touch and

make love? Or was that to be the end of what might have
grown into a lifetime commitment?

Her heart ached and the guilt built until she thought she'd
go crazy. It had started out as a harmless gesture. She had so
much wanted to pretend she led a carefree, exciting life. The
clothes had made the difference. Wearing her sister's clothes
made her feel free and interesting and that she could attract
others to her side.

It was as if a spell had broken. Today she donned her own
jeans and plain shirt, and the magic had ended. Cade wanted
nothing to do with her.

Ten

"What was that all about?" Jackie asked a few minutes later when Julianne closed the kitchen door behind her.

"He's mad."

"That, I could tell. Why? Just because you left early?"

Julianne wandered listlessly over to the table and picked up her cup of cold coffee. She hesitated near the microwave, then turned and tossed it down the sink. Maybe she could have warmed it up, but she didn't. Pouring the last bit from the pot, she switched off the machine.

"It's more than that," she said, pulling out a chair and flopping down. Broodingly she stared at her cup, then raised her gaze to her sister. "I blew it big time."

"He'll come around. Sometimes guys are sensitive on the morning after. But if it was any good, he'll be back."

Julianne winced. It had been more than good. Fantastic came to mind. Wonderful. Glorious. Sighing softly, she shook her head.

"You two sure hit it off fast," Jackie commented. "I, er, assume he rings your chimes?"

"God." Julianne tried a shaky smile. "An entire carillon." Twisting her cup, she glanced at her sister. "Cade thought I was you," she said.

"What?" Jackie sat up at that. "What do you mean, he thought you were me?"

Julianne shrugged. "He barged in on me the morning after you left and assumed that I was you and I sort of never told him I wasn't."

"I don't believe it! What do you mean you 'sort of never told him'? What's there to say? 'I'm Julianne Bennet, Jackie's twin sister.'"

Julianne cleared her throat and met her sister's outraged eyes. "Actually, Jackie, there are a few other people around here who think they've seen you this past week." Might as well confess the entire thing.

"You pretended to be me? Why? I don't get it."

"From envy maybe. Or just for fun. I don't know. It seemed harmless at first. It was a bit scary, too. Your life is so different from mine. I wanted a chance to experience it. Really experience it. So I put on some of your clothes. It was as if I put on an entirely new personality. I felt daring, and competent and…and…I don't know. Different. You have so much that you take for granted. Try living in a small town all your life. A small Southern town, where there are traditions galore. Where what the neighbors think counts more than doing what you want to do. Where adventure is hiking the Blue Ridge Trail. Maybe it's the old grass-is-always-greener syndrome. I don't know."

Jackie looked at her oddly. "Actually I would have loved to grow up in a small town, if someone paid me some attention. I always envied you—you had a stable environment, and siblings to play with and love. Mom. I scarcely know my half-brothers and half-sister. Heck, I hardly know our mother."

Julianne stared. "We're even, I don't know Dad. Though I

did have lunch with him one day. He thought I was you, too,''
she said gloomily.

Jackie laughed. ''That's not surprising. He can't see beyond
his nose, unless he's holding a script in hand. So you pretended to be me. What did you do?''

Julianne spent the next few minutes relating her week in
California. Jackie found it hilarious and laughed frequently.
Once or twice Julianne caught a glimmer of amusement, but
every time she mentioned Cade, guilt and depression reared
up. She couldn't excuse the seductive lure of pretending to be
someone else as a lark anymore. She had lied and a man had
thought he was falling for her. How could she have been so
stupid?

''So now he's furious, and even I can't blame him,'' she
ended. ''Yesterday at the barbecue Phil told me how Cade
hated liars. Cade even mentioned it a couple of times, but I
just couldn't find my way to confess. It's even worse because
of his wife, I guess.''

''I've heard about his wife. She played around on him. She
was frivolous and flighty and pretty as all get-out. He's always
shied away from pretty women since I've known him,'' Jackie
said pensively.

''Well, I'm no beauty.''

''Of course you are. I am, and we're twins.''

Julianne looked at her sister in astonishment. ''Maybe with
the right clothes.''

''Clothes, nothing. Well, maybe they gild the lily. You wear
very bland colors. Our coloring is strong enough for bold
tones. But that's not what makes a person pretty. It's facial
features, and what you do with them. I bet you smiled at Cade
and he was a goner.''

''Hardly. Actually last night was the first time I— Well
anyway, he wanted to earlier, but I held off.''

''He probably did think you were me. We've known each
other a long time, but there's never been anything like that

between us," Jackie said. "Wonder what he thought changed."

"He thought I'd changed, he kept asking me that. Even dressed up in your clothes, I wasn't the same. You have a lot more experience in life than I do."

"You read all the time, don't you? I remember that from when we were kids. You thought reading was the most fun you could have."

Julianne nodded, twisting the cup around and around. "I still like to read. So all my experience is secondhand, from books. I just wanted to do something different while I was here, while I was on vacation. I feel like I was exciting for the first time in my life. Like I could be free and enjoy things and not have to worry about tomorrow and all the mundane things about life."

"What happened to David?" Jackie asked.

Her sister glanced up. "One look at Cade Marshall and I knew I could never settle for David," she answered honestly. "I called him the next day and told him I could not marry him. Not that I had a chance of a marriage with Cade. But he made me see that settling for David was not enough. If nothing else, I'll always be grateful I didn't make that mistake."

"Give the man a break. Let him cool off, then go talk to him."

Blinking back tears, Julianne shook her head. "He doesn't want to see me again. Oh, Jackie, I've made such a mess of things. I'm in love with a man who never wants to see me again." The tears spilled over and this time Julianne made no attempt to stop them.

Cade drove his car as if the demons of hell chased him. Porsches were built for speed, aerodynamically sound on turns and straightaways; and he pushed the car to its limit. Anger fueled his driving. He'd stormed out of his house moments after slamming the door on Julianne. Furious, he'd gotten behind the wheel and took off. Driving up the coast usually soothed him when stress and complications from work built up. He'd thought he'd find the same kind of relief today.

But the anger that had boiled over that morning had merely turned to a slow simmer. He'd like to throttle Julianne Bennet. She'd played him for a fool, smiling her innocent smile and lying through her teeth! He couldn't decide if he were more angry with her, or with himself for falling for her. There had been a dozen signs, he realized, if he had just followed up on them. She'd asked him what to wear to dinner that first night. Jackie would never trust a man's judgment about fashion. Julianne had enjoyed sitting quietly on the beach, Jackie was one for bright lights and action. Suddenly he remembered her comment about Virginia Beach. Was that where she was from?

A glimmer of perverse admiration peeked out. She had pulled off the charade perfectly. He'd only thought Jackie had changed a little, or he himself had. For not knowing her way around Malibu, she'd done all right. Even fooled Jackie's friends at Garcia's that first night.

Not that it changed anything. She had lied. Dammit, he *hated* that. Hated that he had come to care for another liar. Hadn't Crystal been enough? Was he destined to fall for beautiful women with black hearts? He should swear off women for good and just forget finding someone to build a life with. Take what they had to offer and be done with it. Maybe there was part of his father in him. Maybe he couldn't stay with someone throughout a lifetime. Would that lead him to deliberately take up with women he knew would not stay the course?

The sun beat down on the road, heat waves shimmered as he roared up the coast highway. One eye on the rearview mirror for cops, he sped along, weaving around slower cars, longing for the peace he usually found on this stretch of road. The hills to the east rose and fell with irregular beauty. The ocean glittered beneath the sun, looking like a sparkling carpet that stretched to the horizon.

He was almost in Santa Barbara before he could think

clearly. Slowing as he approached the outskirts, he began to look for a place to eat. He was still angry, but hunger pangs were beginning to make themselves felt. Finding a small café near the beach, he parked the car and walked back. There were no cliffs here, the road was practically on the white sand. Pausing a moment, Cade stared out to sea, letting the pristine setting calm him.

As he ate, he thought about what he wanted to do. Despite everything, he still wanted Julianne Bennet. He was a fool. Yet, he wondered if he would ever get over the shock of finding he'd been her first lover. Her inexperienced hands had about driven him mad as she'd tried to undress him. Her wide-eyed innocence had proved to be no act. And her own surprised delight at the pleasure they shared drove away some of the chill surrounding his heart. He had almost changed his mind about staying away from beautiful women.

He had thought Julianne different from Crystal, different from other women with their eye to the main chance. Just when he had thought to give it another shot, he discovered she wasn't even who he thought she was.

Cade spent the day in Santa Barbara. He had nothing waiting at home, did not plan to go into the office, the turmoil he felt would make him useless for anything creative. He wandered around the older part of town, ate at another beachfront restaurant, this one overlooking the small boat harbor. In the afternoon, he sat on one of the benches near the beach and watched the waves crash over the white sand. When he got too hot, he moved to another location with shade. All through the day, he thought about Julianne. About the time the two of them had spent together. He wanted to wring her neck, and rant and rave at her until she begged him for forgiveness. Swore to never lie to him again. Until she promised to be faithful forever.

Then he'd feel the anger build. At himself for caring what she would do in the future. He wanted nothing to do with a liar. He'd had enough with Crystal. A leopard wouldn't change its spots, he was a fool if he thought a woman was any different.

Yet the essence of the woman had not been a lie, had it? Genuine pleasure shone from her eyes at the most innocuous things. She liked walking along the beach, liked sitting quietly for hours and watching the surf. She had been interested in what he told her about his work, her questions intelligent and insightful. He'd wondered at the change in Jackie. There was an inherent *niceness* about Julianne that came through. Surely the feelings between them hadn't been all false. Thinking back over the days they'd spent together, he could sift through what had been pretense and what had been real.

It was long past dark when Cade turned into his driveway. Involuntarily his eyes sought the house next door. Lights blazed from a dozen windows. Of course, Jackie was home. She might even be having a party, for all he knew. He stopped the car and got out. It was quiet, no sounds of music or laughter or people talking. Maybe Jackie just liked a lot of light. He had never noticed before. Hadn't paid that much attention to his neighbor.

He turned toward his house, but couldn't go inside. He still felt too raw. Walking toward the cliff, he let his eyes take in the silvery sheen on the ocean. The moon was waning, in another week or so it would be much darker if he wanted to walk along the beach. The brightness dimmed just as it had with Julianne.

When he reached the edge, he noticed a small fire burning to his right, near the base of the cliff. Drawn, he headed for the carved stairs and quietly descended.

A lone figure sat by the fire, gazing into the flickering flames. Julianne. Sitting on a log drawn up near the blaze, she appeared not to hear him as he walked across the soft, still warm sand.

Cade approached slowly. The fire showed evidence of having been burning for quite a while. Had she been out here alone, or had Jackie insisted on an impromptu picnic? He'd seen Jackie a few times, with friends around a campfire, drinking from a huge cooler someone brought down. There were no signs of that now. Just Julianne Bennet and the fire and the empty beach.

As he came into the light of the fire, she caught sight of him. She looked up briefly, then returned her gaze to the fire without saying a word.

The breeze had picked up and the air felt cooler as it buffeted gently against them. The strong tang of salt filled his nostrils until he moved close enough to have her special fragrance mix with that of the sea. He sat beside her on the log. The fire gave off light and warmth, but he wondered if she felt the dampness in the air. Not that he cared; he just didn't want her to get chilled.

"We hunted for driftwood, built the fire and roasted marshmallows over the open flame," she said.

"I've seen your sister do that before. She seems to like it."

Julianne nodded. "I think she finds that very primitive and so it holds a certain novelty. She's obviously never been camping."

He looked at her, shadows dancing in the flickering flame. The glow of the moon had dimmed since the night they had walked along the ocean's edge. Was it a foreshadow of their relationship? It was over. Yet, angry as he was, he still wanted her. Wanted to feel the softness of her hair tangle with his fingers. He wanted to feel her lips against his, taste her sweetness, savor the fragrance that captivated him. How could he still want her when he hated what she'd done? His desire for Crystal had vanished once he'd discovered her perfidy. Now he felt an urge for forgiveness. For clearing the air and seeing if they could— Could what? Work things out? But he couldn't trust her.

"And you've been camping?" he asked.

"Lots of times. We live practically in the Blue Ridge Mountains. My folks have taken us hiking and camping since I was about nine. My stepfather is great for that kind of thing. He loves fishing in mountain streams.''

"I know nothing about Julianne Bennet," Cade said.

"I know." She turned away slightly, hunching closer to the fire.

Cade reached out and cupped her chin, turning her face to his. Her eyes were swollen. Had she been crying? Something loosened inside. "Tell me something about her."

She blinked furiously and jerked her head away from his hand. "Jackie and I are twins. Our folks split when we were seven. Since then I've lived with Mom in Virginia. She remarried about a year or two after the divorce. I have two stepbrothers and a stepsister. I'm a librarian."

He waited, but she offered nothing more.

"Where do you live in Virginia?"

"Charlottesville. It's a pretty place, but miles from the ocean. I like it here, I feel like I'm on the edge of the world." Her voice was faint, wistful. "I'm sorry, Cade. Sorry I didn't tell you who I was at the very beginning. But I couldn't believe at first that you could think I was Jackie. Then I thought you only stopped by each time because you thought I *was* Jackie. I didn't think you'd find me very interesting."

"We'll never know, will we? Where's Jackie?"

"She went to see if she could find some more marshmallows.''

He heard the tears in her voice and deliberately hardened his heart. Crystal had used similar tactics to try to explain her motives, excuse her behavior. He hated a woman in tears. It made him feel so ineffective. But he would die before letting Julianne Bennet know that.

When she reached out and touched his arm, he looked at her.

"Cade, I never meant to deceive you. I just wanted you to know that. And how much I enjoyed spending time with you. I'll have wonderful memories of my visit to California. I never meant to hurt you. Pretending to be Jackie was childish and foolish. It started out as make-believe, and then got out of hand. I feel so badly about that.''

''I imagine everyone who gets caught feels that way.''

''No, it's not just because you found out. I tried to tell you last night. I left your place this morning with the intent of finding a way to tell you that maybe wouldn't make you so mad. The last thing I want is for you to be upset. I want only happiness and joy for you.''

''You could have fooled me.''

She swallowed hard and met his gaze bravely. ''I was falling in love with you, I think. I wouldn't have hurt you for the world. It was not deliberate on my part. I didn't start out thinking 'let's see if I can fool Jackie's neighbor.' But you thought I was her when we first met, and I've thought she led such an exciting life. I wondered if I could fool someone into thinking plain shy Julianne Bennet was really her sophisticated worldly sister. And then it just kept going and going.'' She tightened her fingers slightly. ''I'm truly sorry.''

''You have a funny way of showing love,'' he said.

''How would you have me show you?'' she asked, leaning just a little closer.

His eyes narrowed. ''Despite everything, I still want you, cupcake,'' he said.

He could see her swallow hard, her eyes searching his in the uneven firelight.

''I want you, too,'' she whispered. Slowly she leaned forward until her lips were a hairbreadth away from his. Cade remained still. How far would she take this? When she closed the distance and kissed him, he knew he'd take whatever she offered, even one more night of passion. He wanted her with an intensity that shocked him.

He wrapped his arms around her slight body and pulled her into his lap. His lips responded to her tentative foray with a mastery of experience. Without prompting, she opened to him and held him close. Blood pounded through him as he sought oblivion to reality with the fiery heat of passion. She tasted sweet and warm and desirable. Her soft body melted against his, even as he felt the swelling in her breasts, her nipples pushing against his chest.

Threading his fingers through her silky hair, he tilted her back to gain access to that tantalizing pulse point at her throat. He kissed her, licked, nipped, and the surging desire rose higher and higher. Her hands slipped beneath his shirt and she traced the contours of his muscles. Stomach tightening, he knew he couldn't wait to get her up to a bed.

Pulling back a scant few inches, he looked into her eyes, blazing with heat. "Are you sure you want this?"

"Very much." Her voice was throaty, low, sexy.

"Sand can get into the damnedest places."

"There's a blanket somewhere. We sat on that first, then pulled the log over." She glanced around the deserted beach. "Jackie might come down." Turning back, she kissed his jaw, rubbing her fingers over his back, around to his taut belly.

He rose, holding Julianne and turned back toward the deepest shadows of the cliff. Scanning the beach, he saw the dark bundle of a blanket. He set Julianne on her feet and quickly yanked up the blanket. Shaking the loose sand from its folds, he took her hand and led her into the shadows near the base of the cliff.

"I'd rather do this by the water's edge," he murmured as he kissed her gently. "I like it when you are bathed in moonlight."

Julianne said nothing, but her hands and mouth answered. She began to unfasten her shirt. When the buttons were free, she shrugged out of it, never breaking their kiss. Cade ran his hands up over her shoulders, down her back, memorizing the feel of her satiny skin against his palms, against his fingertips. He was surrounded by the scent of her, it filled his nostrils and blossomed in his mind. He'd forever remember this night.

When she unzipped her jeans, he sat back on his knees and watched as she pushed them down and stepped out of them.

Dainty and delicate were the thoughts that crowded. Then he forgot everything except his need for this woman.

She watched him from shy eyes. Her innocence still drove him crazy. If he made love to her a million times, would she still have this power? Or would one day he grow used to her and find she'd lost the enchantment? She was no longer totally innocent, yet the aura clung to her. Some of it was a state of mind, not a state of body. Though right now all he could think about was the state of his body and the proximity of hers.

She reached out and unfastened the snap on his jeans and he grew painfully harder. In defense, he stripped his clothes off before her gentle fumbling drove him over the edge. He wanted to savor every minute.

When he reached for her, she flowed into his arms, her mouth warm and welcoming, her body ready for his. Slowly he laid her on the blanket, resting by her side, his hand caressing, touching, reveling in her responses. The tempo built between them and soon she breathed as rapidly as he, her hands almost frantic with need and desire.

When he covered her, he held totally still for a moment, imprinting the feel of her slight frame beneath his. Her breasts pressed hard, her legs were silky as they cradled him. Surging into her heat, he almost stopped, the pleasure was so intense. But it would build, he knew that, and slowly he set the rhythm that would take them to the summit and over.

The cool evening air blew across them, the soft surge and flow of the surf filled their ears, and the scent of love mingled with their own. Higher and higher the tension built, stronger and stronger the desire for completion, until finally with one last surge, Cade felt the convulsions surrounding him, knew from her soft cries that she'd reached the summit, and he allowed himself to follow immediately.

Sand is not as forgiving as a bed, so he rolled off as soon as he could. He did not want to have it end uncomfortably. Spent, he lay on his back, feeling the cool breeze dry his damp skin. It didn't take long for the heat to dissipate and a chill to replace it. He had to get up and get dressed. But in a minute. For now it was enough to lie on the blanket next to Julianne, stare at the dark sky and drift.

Julianne sat up first. She glanced at him, and then reached for her clothes.

"I'm cold," she said softly.

"It doesn't take long for the air to cool things down," he agreed, sitting up. He raised one knee and rested an arm on it while he watched her dress. Even putting on the clothes, she seemed alluring. Dare he take time to remove them once more? He would miss her. How could he let her go?

She shivered a bit and, fastening her shirt, walked out of the shadow to the dwindling fire. The warmth welcomed her and she stood close. Jackie had not returned. Had she seen them and discreetly stayed away? For a moment Julianne toyed with the idea of adding some more wood, but decided against it. Time enough to let it die. It was getting colder and there was no point in remaining just to have a fire.

Cade stepped into the light, fully dressed. The blanket was folded and he held it out to her.

He studied her in the light. Julianne turned away. She was sure she looked a fright. First her eyes were puffy from all the crying she'd done that day. Now her hair probably looked like something a cat dragged through the brush. She wrapped her hands in the blanket, the only warmth coming from the fire.

"Goodbye, Julianne Bennet," he said slowly.

Julianne spun around. "Goodbye?" Involuntarily she glanced at the base of the cliff where not ten minutes before they had made love. Had it meant nothing to Cade? "I thought, I mean, after—" She gestured vaguely toward the shadow.

"It was fine, but changed nothing, did it? Unlike you, I don't lie. I made no promises to you. You offered. I still wanted you and so I accepted your offer."

"End of discussion," she said painfully. Tilting her chin, she faced him.

"Goodbye, Cade Marshall. I hope you aren't crushed to discover one day that everyone is not as perfect as you. Or maybe you'll find that paragon of a woman and marry her and live happily ever after. But I bet she'll never love you as much as I do. As much as I did!" She corrected herself. Without waiting another minute, she headed for the stairs. Tears blinded her, but she could make out the general shape of the stone steps. Once she reached the first one, she climbed them easily, the blanket held tightly against her chest like a shield.

Julianne almost ran across the yard, into the kitchen. Dumping the blanket near the door, she continued without pause. Jackie sat in the living room, soft music playing in the background as she leafed through a magazine. She raised her head as Julianne came into view.

"I saw you had company, so I didn't come down," she said.

"It might have been better if you had," Julianne said without slowing. She ran lightly up the stairs. In only seconds she was in her bedroom, the bright light almost hurting her eyes after the darkness at the beach. She sat on the bed and rubbed her eyes. She had been a fool from the get-go and had no one but herself to blame. But, dammit, it hurt! She loved him. Hadn't meant to fall in love, but there it was. And not a thing she could do about it. The fault lay entirely with her.

"Didn't patch things up, I take it," Jackie asked from the door.

"No. He said goodbye for good tonight." She did not need to tell her sister everything. "I guess while he rang my chimes, I didn't ring his." She lay back, her arm over her eyes. Yet why had he wanted to make love with her a second time? She wished her dazed senses would calm down enough for her to think. Was there some way to reach him, to gain his forgiveness and explain how much she loved him?

"Well, no one ever said men were the smartest creatures God ever created. Now what?"

Julianne gave a wistful smile. "I don't know. I ran from

Virginia to get away from David. Now do I run from California to get away from Cade?''

"We could take a few days to see some of the state. You haven't seen much of anything since you've been here and we have a lot to offer here on the West Coast. What do you say?''

Julianne sat up and nodded, determination shining from her eyes. "I say that sounds like a good idea. Let's cram every day so full I won't have time to think about some arrogant prig of a guy that…that I'm crazy about." Tears threatened again, but she swallowed them. "Tomorrow, I want to go to Disneyland."

Jackie laughed and joined her twin on the bed, hugging her hard. "Disneyland it is. After that we can drive up to Napa and spend a day or two tasting all the wine they make there, then go up to Lake Tahoe and spend a few days at Stateline and the casinos. Catch a few shows. You haven't seen San Francisco, that's a jewel of a city."

"I only have two weeks left," Julianne said, suddenly daunted by the activities Jackie rattled off.

"What we don't get to this trip, we can see on another one. This doesn't have to be your only venture to the West Coast, right?''

"Right." But in her heart Julianne knew she would not come back as long as Jackie's next-door neighbor lived there. The memories and might-have-beens would be too strong, too painful. She had to see everything in the next few days and then say goodbye.

Like Cade had said goodbye, maybe with a few regrets but no looking back.

Eleven

"**I**'m too tired to dress up," Julianne complained as she lay across her sister's bed eleven days later and watched as Jackie carefully put on her makeup.

"No, you're not. You had a nap this afternoon, and we did nothing all day but drive home and rest. Come on, get up and get dressed. Wear something of mine. If we had been thinking, we could have bought look-alike dresses."

"Great, so we look like the Doublemint twins? And I ought to wear my own clothes. Wearing your clothes is what got me in trouble in the first place."

"Nonsense. Pick out a wild dress. This is the first time Dad has taken both his grown-up daughters out to dinner. And then we're going to that party in Beverly Hills. Do not embarrass me by looking like a country cousin!"

Julianne nodded, smiling at her sister's teasing. If her heart wasn't in it, she hoped Jackie wouldn't notice. Her twin had done so much over the last week and a half to cheer her up. It wasn't Jackie's fault she was not cheer-up-able. Ruthlessly resisting the urge to glance out the window at Cade's house, she walked into the huge closet and began to sort through her twin's clothes. Bright and bold and daring, that's the image she wanted to portray today. Carefree and fun-loving. She had her whole life before her—to grieve for her lost love. The worst part was, it was all her fault. If she could turn back the clock and change things, she would do so in a red-hot second.

It was her own insecurities that got her in this fix. Maybe Cade would have liked her for herself. If she truly had any hopes of making a life together, she had cheated them both by not letting them find out if the spark between them was because she was Julianne Bennet, not her sister.

She had chastised herself a dozen times every day—while riding the jungle boats in Disneyland, on the cable cars in San Francisco, as they sped along beside acres and acres of vineyards in Napa. She had wanted to share her delight in the beauty of Lake Tahoe with Cade, had wished he'd been the one to order champagne when she'd won the jackpot on the nickel slots.

Each night she'd lay awake long after her sister had fallen asleep, wondering when she could have changed the course of destiny, berating herself for allowing the foolish masquerade to go on too long.

"Wear the hot pink," Jackie called.

Julianne stared at the clothes as if she'd never seen them. Sighing, she shoved a couple of dresses along the rod until she came to the hot pink one. Might as well wear it, if it made Jackie happy. She wondered if she'd ever be truly happy again.

"Okay, let's go wow them!" Jackie said a little later, standing beside Julianne in front of the mirrored wall.

Two peas in a pod. The words echoed in her mind as she gazed at herself and her twin. Her father had called them that many times when they had all lived together. It was still true. Jackie had insisted she use her makeup, brush her hair in a similar style. While the dresses didn't match, one electric blue and one hot pink, the two women who wore them were as alike as two peas in a pod. Would their father make the same remark?

"I hope Dad's not mad that I pretended to be you," Julianne said as they walked down the stairs together.

"Are you kidding, he laughed for five minutes when I told him on the phone this afternoon. He loves things like that. Why not? That's what he does for a living, after all, pretend to be other people. And he sees the joke on himself, not recognizing his own daughter. Of course to hear him tell it now, he suspected something was different. But I think he's proud as punch that you pulled it off. He worried you would turn out too retiring, like Mom."

"Mom? She not retiring. Good grief, she runs half the charities in town. Is active in P.T.A. and the church. And she doesn't put up with any guff from anyone, rambunctious brothers included."

"Maybe she just couldn't share the limelight with Dad," Jackie said, switching on the light in the living room. The sun was setting and bathed the room in its golden rays. The lamp filled the corners of the room with light. "Want something to drink before he gets here?"

"No." Julianne sat on the edge of the sofa, keeping her eyes resolutely away from the window. She was getting over Cade Marshall. She would not act like some teenager and moon around the windows waiting to catch a glimpse of him. She'd enjoy the evening with their father, and then begin packing. She planned to return home the day after tomorrow. Her vacation was almost over, and the last couple of days she'd spend with her family.

Cade pulled into his driveway and stopped. Looking at Jackie du Marcel's home from habit, he was surprised to see lights in the living room. It wasn't full dark yet, but she had turned on lights. They were home. He didn't move for a long moment, curiously numb. For eleven days he'd wondered where they'd gone. Not that he expected to see them, but it was odd that Jackie left and didn't let her neighbor know to watch out for her house. She had always done so when leaving for France, or on a filming somewhere.

Of course she probably took Julianne's side of the matter and thought he was being unreasonable and irrational. Hardnosed and unforgiving. Those were only some of the words Phil had used when he'd heard the entire story. Or as much as Cade had relayed. Phil had laughed and thought it funny. Couldn't understand why Cade took it so badly.

Cade had not told him how betrayed he felt. How he'd just begun to relax the stringent controls he'd placed on his heart when around Julianne. How for a few days he'd begun to hope he could make a life with her, share his work, enjoy her company.

No use thinking along those lines. He'd told her goodbye.

Not that saying the words had changed anything. Even after eleven days without seeing her, he wanted to be with her. Wanted to tell her about Phil's latest assignment, and hear her ask questions that showed she cared. Wanted to talk to her about the new project they'd bid on and received; share walks along the beach. He wanted to touch her, and feel her warmth and delight envelope him. He wanted to see that innocence beaming up at him in honesty.

The real woman had been there all along. Why hadn't he spotted it? Why had he insisted on thinking she was Jackie and not called her on some of the inconsistencies? If she'd confessed earlier, if he'd discovered the pretense immediately, would it have made a difference?

Crashing a fist against the steering wheel, he gave it up. He was stronger than that. He'd gotten over Crystal, he'd get over Julianne Bennet.

But when he climbed from the car, instead of heading inside, he walked across the lawn to Jackie's house.

Knocking on the door, he waited impatiently. He hadn't a clue what he'd say, but he wasn't leaving until he'd seen her.

The door opened and Jackie stood in the frame looking at him. Her gaze was cool, distant. She was dressed in some bright blue dress, diamonds sparkled at her throat and ears. Saying nothing, she just stood there and looked at him, waiting for him to say the first word.

Cade felt like an idiot. He looked beyond her into the house, but couldn't see into the living room from the door. Was Julianne still here? Or had she returned to Virginia?

The silence stretched out.

"I see you are home," he said at last.

"We got back today."

We! So Julianne hadn't left yet. "And going out already?" Jackie always liked to party, that much he knew about his neighbor. He should have seen the difference in Julianne, she'd been content when it was just the two of them.

"Yes." Gone was the lighthearted banter that they had exchanged over the past two years. Only a chilled reception waited.

Her eyes narrowed. "You want to see Julianne?" she asked at last.

It was like touching an aching tooth. He did and he didn't. He shrugged. "Actually, I'm out of coffee, thought I could borrow some. Save me a trip back out to the store." Hadn't that been the reason he'd come over to Jackie's house that day he'd returned from Italy? God, had it been three weeks? His entire life seemed altered.

Jackie opened the door all the way and gestured toward the living room.

When Cade reached the archway, he saw her. She looked just like her sister. If he hadn't known better, he would be unable to tell them apart. The pink dress covered her like a glove, outlining the curves and valleys he knew so well. Her hair swirled around her face, framing it like her sister's. Even the coolness and distance in her gaze matched Jackie's. If they had dressed alike, would he be able to tell them apart? He thought so. There was a primal pull of physical attraction between Julianne and him, missing with her sister.

"Hello, Cade," she said, cool as a cucumber.

"Julianne." He turned to Jackie, still watching Julianne from the corner of his eye. "Where did you go?"

"Julianne's on vacation, so we went sightseeing, of course. I'll get that coffee." Jackie's smug smile did nothing to endear her to him. So what if she saw through his excuse? Had Julianne?

The silence stretched out. Julianne sat back on the edge of the sofa, her gaze on the carpet.

"What did you see?" Cade asked, stuffing his hands into the pockets of his pants.

"We drove to San Francisco, then up to the wine country and on to Lake Tahoe. Jackie says I should come in winter and try skiing." She could have been a stranger for all the inflection in her voice.

The doorbell rang before Cade could respond.

"Excuse me." Julianne circled around him, heading for the door.

"Hello!" Steven Bennet's booming voice filled the room. In seconds he walked in, his arm around Julianne's shoulders.

"Do you know Jackie's neighbor, Cade Marshall?" Julianne asked her father politely.

"We met once before, I believe." The older man nodded to Cade. "Are you joining us tonight?"

"No," Julianne said quickly. "It's just you, me and Jackie."

He laughed. "Did this minx tell you about fooling me? We had lunch a couple of weeks ago and I thought she was Jackie. Alike as two peas in a pod."

Julianne smiled at the words, her father hadn't forgotten.

"She fooled me, too," Cade said slowly, his eyes on her. The repentant woman of eleven days ago was gone. She glowed as she smiled at her father.

"I've heard of twins doing that. Did you two do it as kids

when we all lived together?'' Steven asked, studying his daughter.

"A time or two in Mrs. Savalack's second grade class. Usually Jackie would pretend she was me to escape punishment for something she had done. I remember missing recess one day for her note passing.''

"Hi, Dad.'' Jackie joined them, carrying a small container. She handed it to Cade and went to kiss her father. He studied her, then Julianne.

Cade felt a bit surprised Steven didn't appear to be at all upset about his daughter's impersonation. He seemed to be almost proud of the fact. "What children do is a bit different from grown women,'' he snapped.

"No one got hurt, so what's the harm?'' Steven replied jovially.

For a split second Cade thought he caught a glimpse of pain in Julianne's eyes, but then she flashed a smile as wide as her sister's.

"Right, no harm done. Think how often we might have done this if we had grown up together.''

"I shudder to think. Ready, my dears?''

Cade moved, gesturing with the plastic container. "Thanks, Jackie.'' He hesitated a moment, then walked on past. There was nothing else to say. He'd seen everything he needed to see.

The morning sunshine streamed into the bedroom window as Julianne turned this way and that in front of the mirrors.

"Do you think you can pull it off?'' Jackie asked from her position lounging on the bed. She wore a mint green negligee that revealed more than it concealed.

Tossing her head, flashing a smile as she tilted her chin down and swept her lashes up, Julianne nodded.

"Even a condemned man gets one last request, doesn't he?'' Her eyes sparkled in determination. "And if he refuses, I'm no worse off, right?''

Jackie laughed. "Right. Go get him, tiger."

Julianne grinned. "I studied you every day of our trip. I'm going to think confident, think competent. And he had better listen. But if not, then at least I tried."

"He said goodbye."

"He didn't need to come by last night. And I really thought he was going to stay. Might have if Dad hadn't shown up. I don't for a second believe he was out of coffee. Or if he was, that he needed to borrow some from you."

"So you're going to go over there and do what? Ask for the coffee back, check out his kitchen to see if he was lying?"

Julianne paused and slowly turned to her sister. "If he isn't out of coffee, he would have been lying, wouldn't he? Would he do something like that? He is so adamant against lying."

"A small fib, no big deal," Jackie dismissed.

Julianne gazed off into space. "Maybe to you or me. But it would be interesting to see if he has coffee, wouldn't it? Maybe I can use that as the excuse, coffee patrol. Jackie, I've got to do this. Otherwise I'm leaving in the morning and won't come back."

"I thought you were getting over him. Thought it was just infatuation. Three days into the trip to San Francisco and you stopped crying."

Julianne sighed and sat on the edge of the big bed. "I hoped at one point it might be infatuation, but nothing went away. I have this huge achy hurt where my heart should be. I think about him all the time, want to share things with him. Want to know what he's doing. Several times last night when you and Dad were laughing at something, all I could think about was how much Cade would enjoy that joke. And I wanted to share it with him. I don't think I'm going to get over him soon."

"Too bad he didn't just laugh it off like Dad did." Jackie looked at her sister. "You okay with Dad, now?"

Julianne nodded. "I guess. I enjoyed last night. And when we were dancing at the party, we had a chance to talk. He

said he'd never had much luck with long-distance relation-
ships, but he had always loved me. I watched him last night.
He needs the spotlight and the adulation he gets from crowds.
I don't really suppose he needs another daughter hanging
around. But I'll see him from time to time. At least I know
he loves me—in his own way.''

"Not like most fathers," Jackie murmured.

"No. But it's enough. And I still have Gerald, who's been
the most wonderful stepfather a girl could have. So I'm lucky,
I have two dads.''

"So get lucky with that obstinate man next door.''

She stood up resolutely. "You're right. This is the only way
I can leave. If he really doesn't feel anything for me but con-
tempt, I'll learn to live with it. But his visit last night made
me think there might be something left.''

Maybe it was just wishful thinking, but Julianne had
hatched this plan before falling asleep last night and wanted
to make one last effort. She got herself into the situation, she
had only herself to make it right.

Julianne walked across the grass, quickly, trying to reach
his house before she changed her mind.

The door was open, the screen in place. She rapped sharply.

"Come on in, I'm in the kitchen," Cade's voice called.

She took a deep breath, opened the door and walked quietly
down the hall. A bright smile lit her face as she stepped into
the kitchen. She just hoped he couldn't see how shaky her legs
were.

"Got any coffee for a neighbor, especially since it's ours
to begin with?" she asked breezily. The words almost caught
in her throat. What she would truly like to do is sit and stare
at the man, or throw herself into his arms and kiss him until
tomorrow.

Cade wore cutoffs that rode low on his hips. His bronzed
chest looked a mile wide, the muscles in his arms drew her
gaze, tantalized her fingers. His hair was tousled and there was
a shadow of a beard. She thought he looked wonderful.

"What are you doing here?" he asked, his gaze trailing down her bare legs, back up to her face.

"Sometimes people do things that turn out differently than they expected."

"I've heard the explanation."

"So hear it again. I was all alone in my sister's house, indulging in the harmless fantasy of pretending to be her. Wearing her flashy clothes, driving that wild car, gazing out over the edge of the world. It was fun and totally new to me. I thought she had such a glamorous life. And it's certainly different from mine."

"So you continued the charade—"

"I'm telling this," Julianne interrupted. "Besides, I'm leaving tomorrow morning. If you don't want to see me again, you can rest easy after that."

Cade paused, just a hitch really, as he reached for a cup. Continuing the motion, he took one from a cupboard and filled it with hot coffee. "So?" he said. "You probably can't wait to get home."

Julianne was a bit disappointed at the reaction. She had hoped for more. "Maybe. At least David will be glad to see me," she muttered.

Cade spun around. "Who is David?"

She shrugged and tried to act nonchalant, tilting up her chin defiantly. "He is the man who asked me to marry him before I came to California." Not every man thought she was a pariah.

"God, so you not only fooled all of us, you cheated on your fiancé!"

"No!" Julianne almost screamed in frustration. She had hoped to spark some jealousy in the man, not have him jump to conclusions that she was just like Crystal. "No, I told him that I could not possibly marry him."

"Because you thought to flush up a better prospect?" Cade said sardonically, shoving the cup of coffee across the counter toward Julianne, as if he couldn't bear to hand her the cup directly.

Julianne reached for it and managed one sip. Placing it carefully back on the counter, she hoped he didn't notice how nervous she was. This wasn't going at all as she had wanted.

"I think you are being unreasonable."

He advanced on her. "I'm unreasonable?" Stopping so close he almost touched her, he drew a breath to continue. His eyes peered deep into hers, his entire body seemed on the alert. "I don't believe this!" he said softly. "You're trying to put some of the blame on me!" He stepped forward and Julianne backed away from the glint of anger that appeared in his eyes.

When she reached the wall, she pressed into it as if to push herself through. He placed a hand on either side of her, fencing her in. There was no place to turn, to run. She could only stand still and face the music.

"Well, it's true. You believed what you wanted to believe. You even questioned me a couple of times. But instead of pushing the issue, you reveled in what there was between us. The glamorous Jackie du Marcel consorting with you. You are so hung up on surface things you never looked below it. Get off your high horse and look beneath. I think you just want a way out. It's much safer that way, isn't it, Cade? Don't forgive me, cut the tie that binds and move on with life."

She pushed against his chest, he was like an immovable wall. Her hand registered the warmth of his muscles long before her brain could think. Heartbeats pounded against her palm. Heat enveloped her. Swallowing, she bravely met his gaze.

Licking dry lips, she cleared her throat. "I wanted to see you again before I left," she said. "I had to see you once more."

She slowly moved her hand until her fingertips rested on his arm, rubbing against the taut muscle, the warm sleek skin. "I know you didn't want to see me again," she said, looking into his green eyes. "You said goodbye the other night at the beach. I thought it was final. You sounded final. But then you came over last night. And for a minute, just a minute, mind you, I thought maybe you had something else to say to me. Then Dad came and the moment was gone. So I thought I'd come over and give us that moment. Only if you don't have a moment for me, then I guess I'll leave.''

He rested his forehead against hers. "You are driving me out of my mind, do you know that, cupcake?''

"Cade, I'm so sorry I didn't tell you right away who I was, but please understand why I didn't. Don't condemn us both to endless, lonely lives because of my one screwup. Forgive me and get to know me and see if you can come to care for me as Julianne Bennet. I truly love you, Cade Marshall.''

"Dammit, I wanted to push you out of my thoughts. I am furious at being played for a fool. But for the past eleven days, you were all I thought about. I didn't know where you were, or what you were doing. There was no way to contact you. So instead, I was forced to remember every moment we spent together. I wanted to see you again. I wasn't sure if I wanted to wring your neck or kiss you silly, but I wanted to see you again. And I already know what Julianne Bennet is like. I spent days with her. Maybe I do need to take some of the blame. I knew you were different from Jackie. She and I have been neighbors for years, I knew something was different, but I didn't want to push it.''

She shook her head slowly, rubbing her forehead against his. "Jackie tried so hard to make my vacation a success. And all I could do was wonder what you would think about the wine, or the shows at the casinos. I don't think I'll ever get over you. Can I do anything to make it right between us, Cade? I'm so very sorry.''

He sighed and closed his eyes. "I feel so strongly about lies because of the hell Crystal put me through. Then I met you and the walls I'd built began to crumble. Maybe I liked that. Maybe I wanted something to change my life. How can I judge it when I'm guilty of a lie, too.''

"The coffee?" she asked, hope beginning to blossom.

"The coffee—oh, damn! That makes two."

"Two lies? From you? I don't believe it." The blossom opened just a bit.

"When you apologized for hurting me, I said I wasn't hurt, just mad. But I found that once the initial anger abated, what lingered was hurt—aching and painful. I was falling in love with you, Julianne. I trusted you and wanted you. God knows how much I wanted you. I thought we were building something wonderful."

"We were. We can. I promise I'll never lie to you again! Oh, Cade, please." Her hands gripped his arms, as her heart began to pound. "I was falling in love, too. And I knew it. You were so different from David. One look at you and I was gone for the count. I promise I'll never lie again no matter what!"

He stared into her eyes. Julianne held her breath. The most important decision of her life was out of her hands. He had to believe her. Had to trust in their feelings enough to give her a chance. He just had to!

"So the first vow we make will be no lies between us?" he said slowly, tentatively.

"I promise. No more lies."

"And no more masquerades!"

"Never again," she said, still afraid to believe things might be all right. Would one wrong word have him sending her away forever?

His lips covered hers and he dropped his hands from the wall to pull her into his arms. Surging against him, Julianne's love for Cade blossomed. Her heart expanded while joy pulsed through her veins.

He pulled back. "I want you. I have wanted you every night since that night on the beach. Hell, I've wanted you since I saw you in that terry-cloth robe."

She groaned. "I hate that robe, I'm getting rid of it."

"Never. I like it. I like your bathing suit and that sexy blue-green dress you wore to dinner. And I like you best in moonlight, nothing but moonlight.''

"Oh, Cade, I love you so much. I'll spend my whole life loving you!'' Her arms tightened and she kissed his jaw, trailing kisses until she reached his mouth.

"I can't wait another minute," he said.

"Well, I sure don't want to," she whispered against his mouth.

"Come with me." He laced his fingers through hers and led her through the house. The bedroom sparkled in the bright sunshine. With the windows open the scent of the sea invaded the room, bringing in the wide outdoors. Cade yanked back the coverlet and turned to her, eyeing her with a hint of uncertainty.

"I knew there was something different when I met you. I never felt anything for your sister, and I can't stop my feelings for you. I love you, cupcake," he said as he pulled her slowly into his arms. His warmth captivated her, his strength supplemented hers. Julianne felt safe, strong and loved.

"I love you, too. I'm not sure I believe this. It feels like magic again. And I was so afraid it had vanished. I'll spend the rest of my life proving my love, I promise.''

Slowly he bunched her shirt up, pulling it over her head. Taking a moment to study the plain serviceable white bra, he smiled as he reached around to unfasten it. "I think this may be more erotic than lace and satin," he said as he slowly slid it down her arms and let it drop on the floor, his eyes devouring her as more and more skin was revealed.

"I've never been one for exotic underwear," she said breathlessly, rubbing her hands against his chest, fascinated by his reaction to her touch. By her own reaction to being so close.

"It doesn't matter, I like you better out of it." Slowly he slid the shorts down her long legs, kissing lightly in passing. First the swell of one breast, the tip of the other, the indentation in her belly, the soft curls that were revealed.

Shivering, Julianne stepped out of the last of her clothes, and reached for his zipper.

When Cade was as naked as she, he scooped her up and whirled her around twice before lying her on the bed. Exuberance shone from his eyes. "You're mine!" he declared as he lay down beside her and reached over to kiss her.

"For as long as you want," she agreed.

He paused, his hand resting on her breast. "I want forever, Julianne Bennet. I want you to stay here in California. To marry me, to live with me and share your life with mine. No lies, no pretenses, just honest love. From me to you and from you to me." His green eyes shone into hers, his voice solemn.

She felt the threat of tears and blinked hard to drive them away. "There's nothing I'd like more. I love you, Cade. I have from that first day."

"Then clear up who this David is." Slowly he traced circles around her nipple, his thumb teasing it from time to time.

She moved, almost unable to think with the cascade of sensations that swept through her. Slowly she reached up for him. "David is no one important to us. He was a friend of mine who asked me to marry him before I left Virginia. But I couldn't say yes. Once I met you, I knew why. There has to be more to life than what David and I shared, and I discovered all of it with you."

The last word was muffled as his mouth covered hers. Her fingers traced patterns across his skin as flames raced through her veins. The heat of the day paled compared to the heat between them. Kisses and caresses, love words and love play mingled. Higher and higher they rose until they reached the crest and flew together to the ecstasy that bound them.

Julianne felt as if she floated on clouds. The soft murmur of the ocean, the call of the gulls, soothed her as her breathing returned to normal. Without the harsh bed of sand beneath her, Cade didn't feel compelled to move away so quickly. She cherished the intimacy, the feel of his hard body against every inch of hers, his breath blowing against her, his hands still caressing her. Their lovemaking was glorious. She wondered if anyone else had ever experienced the full wonder she found with this man. Smiling softly, she brushed her chin against his shoulder.

"Am I too heavy?" he asked, turning to kiss her earlobe.

"No. I like this."

"I like it, too, cupcake."

"That's the other thing," she said a minute or so later, her hand tracing random patterns on his back. She didn't want to move. Only tied so closely together could she convince herself the separation was over, that they would be together forever.

"What?"

"You rarely called me Jackie. Sometimes I would almost forget that I was playing a part. I was myself, except when going out places. I'm not use to parties and wild living. I always felt special when you called me cupcake."

He pulled back and stared into her eyes. "You didn't seem like Jackie, at least the neighbor I'd known for two years. You looked like her, wore her clothes, but something was different from that first morning. I thought of you as different, so maybe that's why I liked the nickname. Maybe we should forget Jackie and Julianne and stick with cupcake."

She smiled and reached up to kiss him. "Suits me. I love you, Cade Marshall."

"And I love you, cupcake." He kissed her hard on her mouth. "Shall we head for Vegas and tie the knot?"

"Are you crazy? My mother would have a fit if I didn't have a traditional wedding with all the trimmings. We'll have to go home to Virginia and have all the trappings. My family's from the South, you know. There are traditions and customs that must be observed."

"What have I gotten myself into?"

"Love?"

"Love!" he concurred. "So be it. Call her today and set a date soon. And you can just plan to stay here until we go back for the wedding. These past eleven days have been hell, I don't want you to leave again.''

Julianne thought wistfully of the quiet life she had led in Virginia, the differences between then and now. Nothing would ever be the same with Cade. Gratitude and love filled her heart.

She would live on the edge of the world with the only man who rang her every chime. Life was perfect!

*   *   *   *   *

When glamour twin Jackie du Marcel visits her sister's hometown will she find forever love or just a fling with THE OLDER MAN, available August 1998 from Silhouette Desire.

Catch more great

HARLEQUIN™ Movies
™

featured on **the movie channel** tmc

Premiering July 11th
Another Woman
Starring Justine Bateman and
Peter Outerbridge
Based on the novel by Margot Dalton

Don't miss next month's movie!
Premiering August 8th
The Waiting Game
Based on the novel by *New York Times*
bestselling author Jayne Ann Krentz

If you are not currently a subscriber to
The Movie Channel, simply call your
local cable or satellite provider for more
details. Call today, and don't miss out
on the romance!

 **the movie channel** tmc  **HARLEQUIN®**
Makes any time special ™
®

100% pure movies.
100% pure fun.

Heat up your summer this July with

Summer Lovers

This July, bestselling authors Barbara Delinsky,
Elizabeth Lowell and Anne Stuart present three
couples with pasts that threaten their future happiness.
Can they play with fire without being burned?

FIRST, BEST AND ONLY
by Barbara Delinsky

GRANITE MAN
by Elizabeth Lowell

CHAIN OF LOVE
by Anne Stuart

Available wherever Harlequin and Silhouette books
are sold.

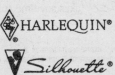

HARLEQUIN®

Silhouette®

HREQ798

MATERNITY LEAVE

Coming September 1998

Three delightful stories about the blessings
and surprises of "Labor" Day.

TABLOID BABY by Candace Camp

She was whisked to the hospital in the nick of time....

THE NINE-MONTH KNIGHT
by Cait London

A down-on-her-luck secretary is experiencing
odd little midnight cravings....

THE PATERNITY TEST by Sherryl Woods

The stick turned blue before her
biological clock struck twelve....

*These three special women are very pregnant...and very
single, although they won't be either for too much longer,
because baby—and Daddy—are on their way!*

Available at your favorite retail outlet.

International bestselling author

JOAN JOHNSTON

continues her wildly popular Hawk's Way
miniseries with an all-new, longer-length novel

THE SUBSTITUTE GROOM

HAWK'S WAY

August 1998

Jennifer Wright's hopes and dreams had rested on her summer wedding—until a single moment changed everything.
Including the *groom*. Suddenly Jennifer agreed to marry her
fiancé's best friend, a darkly handsome Texan she needed—
and desperately wanted—almost against her will. But U.S.
Air Force Major Colt Whitelaw had sacrificed too much to
settle for a marriage of convenience, and that made hiding
her passion all the more difficult. And hiding her biggest
secret downright impossible...

**"Joan Johnston does contemporary Westerns
to perfection."** —*Publishers Weekly*

Available in August 1998
wherever Silhouette books are sold.

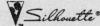

HERE COME THE

Virgin Brides!

*Celebrate the joys of first love with more
unforgettable stories from Romance's
brightest stars:*

SWEET BRIDE OF REVENGE
by Suzanne Carey—June 1998 (SR #1300)

Reader favorite Suzanne Carey weaves a sensuously powerful
tale about a man who forces the daughter of his enemy to be
his bride of revenge. But what happens when this hard-
hearted husband falls head over heels...for his wife?

THE BOUNTY HUNTER'S BRIDE
by Sandra Steffen—July 1998 (SR #1306)

In this provocative page-turner by beloved author
Sandra Steffen, a shotgun wedding is only the beginning when
an injured bounty hunter and the sweet seductress who'd
nursed him to health are discovered in a remote mountain
cabin by her gun-toting dad and *four* brothers!

SUDDENLY...MARRIAGE!
by Marie Ferrarella—August 1998 (SR #1312)

RITA Award-winning author Marie Ferrarella weaves a
magical story set in sultry New Orleans about two people
determined to remain single who exchange vows in a mock
ceremony during Mardi Gras, only to learn their bogus
marriage is the real thing....

*And look for more VIRGIN BRIDES in future months,
only in—*

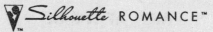

Silhouette ROMANCE™

Available at your favorite retail outlet.

Look us up on-line at: http://www.romance.net

SRVBJ-A

MEN at WORK

All work and no play?
Not these men!

July 1998
MACKENZIE'S LADY by Dallas Schulze

Undercover agent Mackenzie Donahue's
lazy smile and deep blue eyes were his best
weapons. But after rescuing—and kissing!—
damsel in distress Holly Reynolds, how could
he betray her by spying on her brother?

August 1998
MISS LIZ'S PASSION by Sherryl Woods

Todd Lewis could put up a building with ease,
but quailed at the sight of a classroom! Still,
Liz Gentry, his son's teacher, was no battle-ax,
and soon Todd started planning some
extracurricular activities of his own....

September 1998
A CLASSIC ENCOUNTER
by Emilie Richards

Doctor Chris Matthews was intelligent, sexy
and *very* good with his hands—which made
him all the more dangerous to single mom
Lizette St. Hilaire. So how long could she
resist Chris's special brand of TLC?

Available at your favorite retail outlet!

MEN AT WORK™

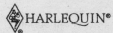 

Look us up on-line at: http://www.romance.net   PMAW2

The World's Most Eligible Bachelors are about to be named! And Silhouette Books brings them to you in an all-new, original series....

World's Most Eligible Bachelors

Twelve of the sexiest, most sought-after men share every intimate detail of their lives in twelve never-before-published novels by the genre's top authors.

Don't miss these unforgettable stories by:

Dixie Browning

MARIE FERRARELLA

Jackie Merritt

Tracy Sinclair

BJ James

RACHEL LEE

Suzanne Carey

Gina Wilkins

VICTORIA PADE

MAGGIE SHAYNE

Anne McAllister

Susan Mallery

Look for one new book each month in the **World's Most Eligible Bachelors** series beginning September 1998 from Silhouette Books.

Silhouette®

Available at your favorite retail outlet.